GANG WAR

Havoc instantly pivoted and executed the *Kinteki-seashi-geri*, kicking his right instep into the Brother's testicles. The blow made Sheba grunt and drop to his knees. Havoc whipped his left hand down, his index finger extended, delivering an *Ippon-nukite* strike to the temple, his bony finger the equivalent of a blackjack.

Stunned, Sheba sagged, his hands holding his groin.

"Hold this," Havoc said, and tossed the M.A.C. 10 to Jaguarundi, who deftly caught the weapon.

"Hit the scumbag again!" Gloria urged.

Havoc reached down, gripped the Brother's chin, and snapped the man's head up so he could glare into Sheba's eyes. "No more games, asshole. I'm tired of being treated like a lightweight. This is the Force you're dealing with, you stupid son of a bitch. If you don't give me the answers I need, Jag here will do to you what he did to your friend."

Also in the BLADE series by David Robbins:

#1: FIRST STRIKE
#2: OUTLANDS STRIKE
#3: VAMPIRE STRIKE
#4: PIPELINE STRIKE
#5: PIRATE STRIKE
#6: CRUSHER STRIKE
#7: TERROR STRIKE
#8: DEVIL STRIKE

#9: L.A. STRIKE

DAVID ROBBINS

LEISURE BOOKS   NEW YORK CITY

Dedicated to . . .
Judy, Joshua, and Shane.
And to all the people I
inconvenienced by moving to Oregon
and back again.
Now you know what my missus puts up with
each and every day.

A LEISURE BOOK®

AUGUST 1990

Published by

Dorchester Publishing Co., Inc.
276 Fifth Avenue
New York, NY 10001

Copyright © 1990 by David L. Robbins

All rights reserved. No part of this book may be reproduced or transmitted in any form or by any electronic or mechanical means, including photocopying, recording, or by any information storage and retrieval system, without the written permission of the Publisher, except where permitted by law.

The name "Leisure Books" and the stylized "L" with design are trademarks of Dorchester Publishing Co., Inc.

Printed in the United States of America.

PROLOGUE

Damn it all!

Not now!

The shakes hit her when she was only three steps from her goal, a really bad case, and her entire body began to quiver. The need was so overwhelming that she almost cried out. If she did, she was dead. So she bit down on her lower lip, her teeth drawing blood, and clasped her arms tight about her middle. You can do it! she told herself, and leaned against the brick wall for support.

Just hang in there.

The sounds of traffic wafted up to her on the sluggish, grimy air. She inadvertently glanced down at the ground 15 stories below and almost lost her balance. Dizzy, she closed her green eyes and waited patiently for the shakes to subside.

Somewhere in the distance a siren wailed.

Gradually the trembling subsided and the gnawing hunger abated, but she knew it was only a matter of time before the need struck her again. Move, bitch! she goaded herself, and hurried to the platform at the top of the fire escape, a four-foot-wide strip of metal that swayed when she stepped upon it. Don't let me fall! She mentally pleaded. Not when she was so close.

The sooty gray door stood before her.

Her nervousness mounting, she gripped the doorknob and licked her dry lips. Please let it be open! She twisted, and to her delight the knob turned and the door creaked open an inch. Cautious now, she peeked inside at the plush corridor with its thick red carpet, ornate overhead lights, and paintings adorning the green walls.

One thing was for sure.

The bastard knew how to live in style.

She listened for sounds, dreading that he might be in his condo and not at his club, but the floor was quiet. Her skin prickling, she eased inside and hastened to his door, the only one on the right-hand side, located in the middle of the corridor. Directly across from his brown door was the red door. She looked at the red paint and barely suppressed an impulse to spit on the panel. The sight filled her with so many memories, and very few of them were pleasant.

How could she have been so stupid?

Annoyed, she shook her head to clear her thoughts, her long black hair swaying. Now was not the time for self-recrimination. Now was the time to get her ass in gear before he returned with his spooky bodyguard.

The thought of the Claw made a tingle run along her spine.

She reached into the right front pocket on her faded jeans and withdrew the key. Her fingers quaking, she fumbled at the lock, and finally succeeded in inserting the silver key into the narrow slit. Two seconds later she stood in the condominium, her heart beating in her chest like a scared rabbit's. Swiping the bastard's key that time and having a duplicate made had been the smartest thing she'd ever done! She thought of the bodyguard again and almost changed her mind. Don't think of the Claw! Think about the crack, all that wonderful, sweet crack she would receive for her trouble!

She moved through the spacious, opulent living room to the bedroom on the east side of the condo. The door was ajar, and in three strides she was standing next to the huge water bed and glaring at the mirrors attached to all four walls. In her mind's eye she saw herself on the water bed, naked, receptive to his amorous advances, and she remembered how she'd felt when he'd traced his fingers from her breasts to her thighs. She'd given him the most precious gift she had: herself. And the prick had tossed her aside for a younger bitch!

Revenge would be hers!

Her resolve cemented, she stepped to the center mirror on the north wall, inserted her bright red fingernails into the crack between that mirror and the next one, and pulled. With deceptive ease the mirror swung out on its hidden hinges, and there, exposed to her view, was the large black safe.

She was so close!

Her left hand slid into her left pocket and extracted the slip of paper containing the combination. Taking a deep breath to compose herself, she began whirling the dial in the proper sequence: first right to one, then left to nine, then right to 50, then left to seven, and right to four.

Bingo.

A loud click signified her success, and she wrenched on the thick handle, tugging the heavy door open to reveal the three shelves. Lying on the second shelf were the four familiar blue notebooks, and she scooped them into her arms with all the passion of an ardent lover.

She had them!

Elated, she scrutinized the safe's contents, consisting of piles of miscellaneous papers, drug paraphernalia including two syringes and three baggies, and a stack of bills. She grabbed the money, her green eyes widening, estimating there must be four grand in her left hand.

Why not?

Beaming, she quickly closed the safe and swung the mirror into position, then hastened to the living room. She was halfway across when she heard the voices and her blood seemed to transform into ice.

They were back already!

For an instant she panicked, wondering if she had removed

the key and locked the door, until she touched the back of her right hand to her pocket and felt the hard outline of the key. Terrified, she darted to the sofa positioned near the south wall and moved to one side. If she recalled correctly, there was a narrow space between the back of the sofa and the wall. She knelt and squeezed into the space, scraping her shoulders, and wiggled behind the sofa, accidentally pushing it outward several inches in the process.

Would they notice?

She held her breath, scared to her core, the notebooks and the wad of money clutched to her chest. Thank goodness the bastard always left the lights on! He couldn't stand a darkened room, even when he slept. Just one of his many quirks.

The front door opened and the voices became clear.

"—know what to do when the stupid son of a bitch gets here."

The melodious voice brought a rush of memories: the night they met at Edith's party; the first time they made love; the first time they did drugs together; her eventual addiction and his loss of interest. She frowned and held herself perfectly still, thinking of the bodyguard. The Claw possessed senses like a cat.

"I know what to do, Boss."

That was him! The professional killer! She recognized his deep, raspy voice immediately. How many times had she seen his tinted shades turned in her direction and wondered what he was thinking about? Dozens, at least.

"Good. Then let's attend to business and get back to the China White. Gloria is waiting for me."

Gloria! That scuzzy buffarilla! Gloria was the one who'd stolen him away!

"I don't much like the idea of wasting the sucker here," the Claw mentioned.

Waste? Did he say *waste*? She couldn't believe her ears. What the hell was going on? She heard muffled footsteps, and then the creak of leather as someone sat down in a nearby chair. The bastard liked leather furniture. All four chairs and the sofa sported the best Corinthian leather money could buy.

"Can I get you anything, Boss?" asked the Claw.

"Not now. I need my mind sharp. Curtis won't go down easy."

The name rang a bell. Curtis Jenson, the dealer who handled a twelve-block territory on the southwest side of Los Angeles. She had talked with him a number of times, and even danced with him once at the annual New Year's bash the bastard threw for all of his people. Not poor Curtis!

"If you don't mind my asking, Boss, why are we doing him here? Why not take him down on the street?"

"My dear Claw, Curtis is no fool. He's one of the smartest dealers in my organization. We're snuffing him here because this is the last place he'd expect any grief. He'll figure I'd have to be stone crazy to kill him in my own condo."

"How do you want it done?"

"Any way you want. Just don't get any blood on the carpet. I can't abide a messy room."

The Claw laughed, a short bark devoid of genuine mirth. "Your wish is my command, Boss."

"Why don't you fix a boilermaker for Curtis? He'll be here any minute."

"One boilermaker coming up."

She heard the Claw walk to the mahogany bar situated along the north wall, and then the tinkle of a bottle pouring alcohol into a glass.

"I don't know what I would do without you, Claw. How many years have we been together now?"

"Eight, Boss."

"Eight years. We've come a long way in such a relatively short time, haven't we?"

"Sure have."

"My brains and your brawn. Together, they're an unbeatable combination."

The Claw did not respond for almost 30 seconds. When he did, his tone had softened somewhat. "Spiff tells me that Fayanne has been asking about you."

An electric shock seemed to course through her body at the mention of her name, and she came close to bumping her head against the wall in her excitement and giving herself away.

"So?"

"Just figured you should know, Boss. She told Spiff that she's trying to kick the stuff. Says she wants you to take her back."

Fayanne's eyes widened in astonishment. If she didn't know any better, she'd swear that the Claw actually cared about her. But the prospect was too ludicrous to contemplate. Or was it? The Claw had always treated her with courtesy and respect, but he treated all women in the same manner.

A snort came from the man seated in the chair. "You have a soft spot for that broad, don't you?"

"She never treated me like a freak," the Claw said.

"Fayanne is a bimbo. Always has been, always will be. I wouldn't take her back if she was the last piece of fluff on the planet. She's a loser, Claw. And I don't associate with losers."

Is that right? Fayanne wanted to yell. Well, she was going to teach that arrogant, egotistical lowlife a lesson he'd never forget.

A loud knock interrupted the conversation.

Fayanne listened as the Claw went to the door and welcomed their guest, in reality their unsuspecting victim.

"Hey, Claw. What's happening?" Curtis Jenson said as he entered. "And there's my main man himself."

"Curtis," the man in the chair said flatly.

"Mr. Bad. I'm here like you wanted."

"Decent of you to come," Mr. Bad responded, his tone dripping honey. "Why don't you pull up a chair?"

"Don't mind if I do," Curtis said.

The fool! Fayanne wanted to jump up and warn him, but to do so would be equivalent to committing suicide and she wasn't ready to go that route. Yet.

"So why the special invite?" Curtis inquired.

"We have an important issue to discuss," Mr. Bad answered, then paused. "Before we begin, would you care for a drink?"

"I'm not thirsty."

"How unfortunate. Claw has prepared a boilermaker for you."

L. A. STRIKE

The bodyguard must have been standing behind Curtis's chair with the drink in hand, because he promptly said, "Here you go, Curtis. Enjoy."

"Thanks, Claw."

Fayanne heard a sipping noise.

"Ahhh. That hit the spot," Curtis said. "Now then, what's this all about?"

"Loyalty," Mr. Bad stated.

"Somebody in the Brothers has turned over?"

"So I've heard."

"Who?"

"You."

A prolonged silence followed the accusation, and Fayanne tensed in expectation of a gunshot or the sound of the Claw doing what he did best.

"Are you jiving me?"

"Would I kid about such a grave matter?" Mr. Bad rejoined.

"Where did you ever hear such bullshit?"

"My source is irrelevant. The accusation is not without merit, or I wouldn't give it the slightest attention. Someone has reported to me that you are being disloyal. The claim is that you're about to turn, to go over to the Barons."

Curtis laughed.

To Fayanne, relying entirely upon her hearing to interpret the conversation, the laugh rang false. Oh, Curtis! she thought. How could you be so dumb?

"Someone has been feeding you a line, Mr. Bad," Curtis declared.

"Have they?"

"Sure. I wouldn't be so stupid as to try and double-cross you. I know what would happen if I did."

"You underrate yourself," Mr. Bad said. "You're extremely intelligent, Curtis. Too intelligent, in fact. You've taken a long look at the grass on the other side of the fence, and you've decided it's greener over there."

"No way, man. I'd never cross you," Curtis reiterated, and expelled a long breath. "Is it getting hot in here or what?"

"I'll have Claw open a window in a moment," Mr. Bad offered. "First, though, to business. Where were you one week ago at eleven P.M.?"

"I'd have to think about it. I might have been with one of the whores on Sepulveda Boulevard."

"Or you might have been with Owsley."

Curtis Jenson must have stood up because Mr. Bad suddenly snapped, "Sit down."

"Whoever told you I was with Owsley is a liar!"

"*Sit down*, Curtis." The words were razor sharp and as heavy as steel.

"I'm sitting," Curtis said. "Man is it ever hot in here."

"After all I've done for you, Curtis, I'm disappointed you would see fit to betray me. I was the one who took you in off the streets and trained you, who made you one of my trusted dealers. And now you've thrown that trust back in my face."

"I didn't, Haywood. Really I didn't."

Fayanne flinched. The bastard hated for anyone to use his real name. For some reason he despised the name his parents had bestowed on him at birth: Haywood Keif.

"Then perhaps you can explain this?" Mr. Bad inquired.

Curtis gasped.

"I'd pity you, Curtis, but I find it hard to pity someone who has demonstrated such stupidity."

"Who took this?" Curtis queried, his tone strained.

"Irrelevant."

No one said a word for a full ten seconds, and then Fayanne heard the sounds of a scuffle, a loud gasp, and the thud of a heavy blow. She figured that Curtis must be dead, but she was wrong.

"Another asinine move, Curtis. You persist in compounding your stupidity. Evidently I was mistaken about you. You're not as intelligent as I believed."

"Why am I so hot?"

"Ask Claw."

Instead, Curtis blurted out, "Oh, God! Oh, God! I don't want to die!"

"Very few ever do."

A spasm of violent coughing racked Curtis and he groaned. "You put something in my drink!"

"Arsenic," the bodyguard answered gruffly, then added, as if in explanation, "The boss doesn't want any blood on the rug."

"I'm getting out of here!" Curtis declared.

Again Fayanne listened to a scuffle, only this time the tussle was punctuated by a sharp snap, the unmistakable crack of a man's neck being neatly broken.

"Thank you," Mr. Bad said.

"Anytime, Boss."

"Let's get to the club. This pathetic wretch has delayed me long enough already. Have Dexter and Sheba dispose of the body."

"Will do."

The front door opened and closed, and silence abruptly descended on the condo.

Fayanne waited a minute to be sure they were gone, then squeezed out from behind the sofa and stood. She nearly dropped the notebooks and the money when she saw Curtis Jenson on the floor near a chair, his eyes wide, his head bent at an unnatural angle, his olive suit rumpled, the healthy sheen of his brown cheeks belying his current state. "Oh, Curtis," she said softly, then dashed to the door. A quick check verified the elevator at the north end of the corridor was almost to the ground floor. She slipped out, closed and locked the door, then ran to the fire escape.

Uh-oh.

Now what should she do?

When she had visited the condo earlier in the day and found the bastard wasn't home, she had stood in the corridor with tears trickling down her face, still unable to believe that he had cut off her credit, and she had happened to gaze at the fire escape door. Then and there the idea had occurred to her, how to get her revenge and all the crack she'd ever need, and she had impulsively unbolted the fire escape door and departed using the elevator. Now that her plan had succeeded, she was stuck with the dilemma of how to bolt the door behind her.

There was no way.
Shrugging, Fayanne decided bolting the door didn't matter. She giggled at her triumph and fled into the muggy August night.

CHAPTER ONE

The chatter of automatic gunfire attained a veritable crescendo, causing a flock of starlings roosting in an oak tree a short distance away to take flight in alarm.

His huge arms folded casually across his massive chest, the giant nodded in satisfaction as he watched the six members of the Freedom Force practice their marksmanship with M-16's. Even when he was standing at ease, the giant's bulging muscles emanated an aura of raw, unbridled power and vitality. A comma of dark hair hung above his gray eyes, which narrowed as he concentrated his attention on one of the six. A black leather vest, green fatigue pants, and combat boots served as his attire. Strapped around his slim waist were his ever-present Bowies, twin knives that had saved his life on many an occasion.

The blasting of the M-16's temporarily abated as the shooters expended the rounds in their magazines and went about inserting new ones.

His mouth curling downward, the giant saw the man on the right fumble and drop a new magazine. He uncurled his arms and snapped, "Concentrate, Lobo! You're not concentrating!"

"Says you, sucker," responded the stocky black man. He wore a black leather jacket, a blue shirt, jeans, and knee-high black boots. Only five feet, seven inches in height, he weighed in the vicinity of 190 pounds, none of it flab. He preferred to style his hair in an Afro that crowned his handsome features.

"Cease firing!" the giant commanded, and strode over to the line. "What did you say?"

"Who, me?" Lobo replied innocently.

"Do you think we're playing games here?"

"Oh, boy. Here we go again," Lobo muttered. "Here comes the speech."

The giant straightened and placed his brawny hands on the hilts of his Bowies. "I'm real tired of having you give me grief all the time, Lobo."

"Who's giving you grief, Blade? All I did was drop the lousy magazine and you jump on my case."

"If that happened in a combat situation, you'd be dead," Blade noted. "Why do you think we spend so many hours on the firing range? Why do we spend so much time on the mats practicing our hand-to-hand fighting skills? For the fun of it?"

Lobo sighed and glanced at his five companions, all of whom were regarding him critically. He faced the giant. "Look bro. We've been all through this a dozen times already. I've got the routine down."

"Do you?"

"Where's the beef, anyway? I pull my fair share of the load around here."

Blade stepped up to Lobo. "The beef, Lobo, is that I don't intend to lose another member of this team. The reason I make you practice and practice is so you'll stay alive when we're out in the field."

"I know that—" Lobo began.

"Then try harder," Blade stated sternly, "or I'll send you back to Clan with a note explaining that you have the mentality of a six-year-old."

"You wouldn't."

"Try me."

"Chill out, dude. I gave Zahner my word I'd stick this out for the whole year. If you send me back early, I won't be able to hold my head up in public."

"That's your problem," Blade said. "Shape up or I'm shipping you out."

Lobo shook his head and muttered, "Boy, what a grump."

"I heard that."

"Figures."

Turning, Blade studied the other members of the Force, wondering how many would still be alive when their tour of duty was over.

The Freedom Force had been the brainchild of one of the leaders of the seven factions comprising the Freedom Federation, factions that had banded together under a mutual defense treaty simply to ensure their self-preservation. Scattered pockets of civilization on an insane world, the Federation was devoted to maintaining a vestige of order and culture when all about them lay ruins, abandoned cities and towns, and the savage Outlands where the survival of the fittest was the unwritten law of the land, a legacy of humankind's ultimate folly.

World War Three.

One hundred and six years ago the nuclear Armageddon had finally been launched, proving that mankind's implied claim to possessing intelligence and wisdom had been a sham. By the time the war ended, after all the nuclear missiles and chemical weapons had been employed, after millions upon millions had perished and the environment had been poisoned with radioactive and chemical-warfare toxins, after the fire storms had subsided and the fallout had descended, the once-fertile and lush planet Earth had been reduced to a polluted caricature of its former self.

In the country once known as the United States of America, there were dozens of organized outposts, city-states, and territories under the rule of one group or another, but by far the major portion of the countryside consisted of the violent Outlands. The Russians controlled a belt of land in the East, the mob had taken over Nevada, the Mormons dominated Utah, the autocratic Technics governed Chicago, and there were many, many other groups, most of them intent on conquering even more land.

World War Three had not taught humanity a thing, or so it often seemed to Blade.

The Federation consisted of the more progressive, stable factions. First there was the Free State of California, the only state to retain its administrative integrity after the war. The governor of California, a man named Melnick, had first proposed forming an elite tactical force to deal with threats to the Federation as they arose. Melnick had even gone so far as to have a special facility constructed north of Los Angeles, slightly northwest of Pyramid Lake, where the Force stayed and trained while awaiting assignments. The headquarters compound consisted of 12 acres surrounded by an electrified fence topped with barbed wire and guarded by regular California Army troops. Of all the Federation factions, California perhaps most resembled the prewar society. Of its large cities, only San Diego and San Bernadino were obliterated during the war. San Francisco and Los Angeles were both intact, although both were considerably run-down in comparison to their former greatness.

The next Federation faction that came the closest to resembling prewar America was the Civilized Zone. Composed of the former states of Kansas, Nebraska, Colorado, Wyoming, Oklahoma, and New Mexico and the northern half of Texas and part of Arizona, the Civilized Zone had been created after the U.S. government evacuated hundreds of thousands of its citizens in the Midwest during the war. The region had been subsequently renamed by the dictator who took over after the U.S. government collapsed.

Of the five remaining factions, none were similar to the prewar culture.

A legion of horsemen known as the Cavalry now controlled the Dakota Territory, a throwback to the rugged pioneer days of early America where most of the men wore buckskins and the women were as hardy as their mates.

The former state of Montana was in the hands of the Flathead Indians, who had finally cast off the white man's yoke and reclaimed their land and their ancient heritage.

Another former state, Minnesota, was the home of three Federation factions. First, dwelling in a subterranean city in the north-central part of the state, were the reclusive Moles. Their city, dubbed the Mound, had started as an underground fallout shelter and gradually expanded over the years. Of all the Federation members, they were the least liked, in large measure due to their leader, a domineering egotist named Wolfe.

Also located in Minnesota, in the northwest quarter, were the refugees from the Twin Cities who had resettled in the small town of Halma and designated themselves as the Clan. They had deliberately moved to Halma to be close to the last Federation faction, the one that had helped them relocate, the one regarded as a sort of Utopia by all the rest.

The Family.

Started by a wealthy survivalist who'd constructed a 30-acre retreat on the outskirts of the former Lake Bronson State Park, the Family now numbered over one hundred members. Although they were the smallest faction in terms of sheer numbers, they wielded the most influence in Federation councils. It was the idealistic survivalist, Kurt Carpenter, who had called his followers the Family and christened their compound the Home. He'd instituted an educational and social system designed to ensure every Family member could enjoy freedom in its truest definition. The current Family Leader, Plato, was known far and wide for his sagacity and kindness.

Not all Family members enjoyed such a reputation, especially the 18 who had been chosen to be Warriors, the guardians of the Home who were responsible for defending the Family from any and all dangers. Renowned for their lethal skills, the Warriors were as celebrated in their own right as the Spartans of antiquity, and justly so. One of their number, the head Warrior, was undoubtedly the most famous man on the continent, a man who had traveled from the baking deserts of Mexico to the frigid tundra of Alaska on his missions against enemies of the Family and the Federation, a man whose reputation as a fighter was unmatched in the postwar era, whose twin Bowies were a symbol of hope for all those oppressed by despots. The man that the Russians, the mob, the Technics, and others knew by the name he had selected at his Naming ceremony on his sixteenth birthday, the man future historians would credit with being largely responsible for salvaging the world from its dark age of despair and helping to guide it toward the ultimate destiny of light and life.

Blade.

Totally unconscious of his status—although aware of the many stories told about him around many a campfire, he tended to shrug them off as idle gossip—the young giant now stood studying the Force recruits, each one a volunteer from a Federation faction, who had agreed to serve for a term of one year.

Lobo, whose given name was Leo Wood, hailed from the Clan. During his youthful days in the Twin Cities, he had been a member of a gang known as the Porns. He was street smart and as tough as they came, and his favorite weapon was a NATO, a spring-loaded knife with a four-inch blade that retracted snugly into a slot at the top of the handle.

Standing next to Lobo was Sparrow Hawk, a Flathead Indian. Five-feet-six, he had shoulder-length black hair and brown eyes. His beaded buckskins fit snugly over his powerful physique, except across his wide shoulders and down his thick arms, where the garment had deliberately been designed loosely to allow for unrestricted movement. Slung over his back by means of a brown leather cord tied to the shaft near the steel head and near the blunt end was his prized spear, a weapon that had once belonged to his father. From the left side of his handcrafted leather belt hung a large hunting knife in a beaded sheath.

After Sparrow Hawk came the volunteer from the Cavalry, a lean man dressed in a black frock coat, black pants, and black boots, all of which served to accent his white shirt.

On his head he wore a wide brimmed black hat, and on his right hip was a holstered revolver, a pearl-handled, nickel-plated Smith and Wesson Model 586 Distinguished Combat Magnum. His eyes were hazel, his hair brown. Don Madsen was his name, although everyone simply referred to him as "Dock." Prior to joining the Force, Doc had made his living as a gambler in Rapid City and other frontier towns in the Dakota Territory, where he had also acquired a feared reputation as a consummate gunman.

The fourth person on the firing line was different from all the rest by virtue of her sex and her inexperience. Raphaela was her name, and she had been sent by the Moles to be their recruit. Her still pale complexion from a life spent almost always underground contrasted sharply with her flaming red hair and her striking green eyes. At five feet eight in height, she presented the perfect picture of frailty even though she wore regulation green combat fatiques.

As did the tall man standing to her left, a broad-shouldered professional military officer endowed with the physique of a classical Greek wrestler. He stood six feet, two inches tall, and wore his blond hair clipped short in the military fashion. On his lapels were the insignia signifying his rank of captain. Mike Havoc was his name, and he was the older brother of another Force recruit who had died ten months ago. His clear blue eyes regarded the Warrior rather coldly.

Last in line, and without a doubt the most unique volunteer in the bunch, was the hybrid. Part feline, part human, the creature known as Jaguarundi had been created in a test tube by a genetic engineer. Before the war, genetic engineering had been all the rage among the scientific elite as they vied with one another to see who could produce the most superior mutation. Jaguarundi's creator, a deranged genius who had gone by the title of the Doktor, had bred an entire corps of hybrid assassins by editing the genetic instructions encoded in the chemical structure of molecules of DNA. During the course of the war between the Federation and the Doktor, which had culminated in the first Federation victory, a number of the geneticist's mutants had rebelled against their maker.

Jaguarundi had been one of them. Thin in the extreme, six feet in height, he wore just a black loincloth because clothes made him uncomfortable. And well they should, what with the coat of short reddish fur that covered his entire body from the crown of his oval head to the tips of his toes. His ears were rounded, and his slanted green eyes had vertical slits for pupils. His teeth, revealed whenever he smiled or snarled, were tapered and razor sharp. He had settled in the Civilized Zone after the Doktor was defeated, and he had volunteered to represent them on the Force.

"So are we done with the firing range for the day, or what?" Lobo queried.

The question brought Blade out of his reverie. He sighed and nodded. "For today, but we'll practice marksmanship again tomorrow and I'll expect you to be able to change magazines without dropping one."

Doc Madsen laughed.

"You find something funny, turkey?" Lobo demanded argumentatively.

"What if I do?" Doc responded, his right hand straying close to his Magnum.

"Just askin'," Lobo said.

Blade frowned. The new recruits still had a long way to go before they would mesh as a team. They had survived their first conflict, against the Mexican bandit who had called himself El Diablo, by the proverbial seat of their pants. Although all of them except for Raphaela had prior combat experience to varying degrees, as a unit they were green. He needed to cram as much training into them as he could before they were sent out on another mission.

Jaguarundi cocked his head to one side, then announced, "We have company coming." His voice was low and raspy.

A moment later Blade heard the sound too, the growl of a jeep engine approaching from the south, from the direction of the gate affording access to the Force headquarters. He turned and spied a vehicle, a roofless Army jeep containing two men, the driver and one other.

General Miles Gallagher.

"Oh, goody!" Lobo said, his gaze on the general. "This must be our lucky day. He probably has another assignment for us. I wonder who will get the chance to try and blow us away this time?"

CHAPTER TWO

The jeep sped past the three concrete bunkers situated in the center of the compound and continued to the north, to the firing range only one hundred yards farther. The driver braked, and out hopped a bulldog of a man in an immaculate dress uniform, his crew-cut brown hair and brown eyes adding to the pugnacious impression he conveyed. Initially, Gallagher had opposed the formation of the Freedom Force. An admitted isolationist, he had never believed that California needed to join the Federation. Although he'd objected strenuously, he had agreed to serve as the official liaison between Governor Melnick and the Force. Now he gave them all a brief scan and focused on the Warrior. "How are they shaping up?"

"Hello to you too, General," Blade said.

"Sorry, but you should know by now I'm not one for formality. I believe in getting straight to the point. It's my military background."

"To what do we owe this honor?"

Gallagher reached behind him and pulled a folded newspaper from his right back pocket. "Have you seen the story yet?" He unfolded the copy, the latest of the *L.A. Times*.

Blade nodded. "I read it this morning. Yes, I saw the article about our mission in Mexico." He didn't bother to mention that he still wasn't reconciled to the practice of having each Force assignment detailed in the press. Governor Melnick had instituted the practice, claiming the news reports would help present the Force in a positive image to the people of California, many of whom had entertained the same reservations about the unit as General Gallagher. Blade suspected that the stories had a twofold purpose. They boosted the Force, but they also indirectly boosted the political career of Governor Melnick. During his schooling years at the Home he had learned about the devious politicians who had frequently manipulated those they purportedly represented during the decades preceding World War Three. Not much had changed, he reflected wryly.

"What did you think of the piece?"

"It was well written," Blade said. "The style reminded me a lot of Athena's."

Gallagher did a double take. "It did?"

"Yeah," Blade stated, thinking of Athena Morris, the previous female member of the team, a journalist who had joined so she could report their escapades firsthand and advance her career in the bargain. To the amazement of everyone, including her, she had fallen in love with the former recruit from the Civilized Zone, another hybrid called Grizzly. Tragically, while under heavy sedation for an injury she sustained in Alaska, she had tried to open a hospital window and fallen to her death.

"I don't see any resemblance in style," the general said.

Blade shrugged. "What does it matter? I'm sure Governor Melnick was pleased with the article."

Gallagher's eyes narrowed. "As a matter of fact, he was."

Captain Havoc cleared his throat. "Do you have another assignment for us, sir?"

"Not this time," Gallagher said, and replaced the newspaper in his pocket. He smiled broadly. "I think you'll be happy to hear why I came."

"Bet me," Lobo mumbled.

Governor Melnick came up with the idea," Gallagher said. "In return for your outstanding performance against El Diablo, and as a token of his appreciation for bringing an end to the raids that plagued southern California for decades, he thought you would all like to have a three-day pass so you can relax in Los Angeles."

"What?" Blade said, straightening.

"You heard me," Gallagher declared, still beaming.

"Wow!" Raphaela exclaimed. "I've never been to a big city before."

"I have," Doc said. "They're nothing to rave about."

"Why not?" Raphaela asked.

"There's no varmint like a human varmint," the gunfighter commented. "And cities are full of folks who would slit your throat for the hell of it."

"Really?"

"Don't listen to the dude, Raphaela," Lobo said. "Hicks don't know squat about city life."

"And I suppose you do?" Doc queried testily.

"I was raised in a city, ding-dong. Remember?"

"You were raised in a rat-infested dung heap. No one lived in the Twin Cities except for low-life gang members. You don't know the first thing about city life."

"Oh, yeah?" Lobo countered, wishing he could come up with a wittier retort.

"That's enough," Blade directed, his gaze on the general. "We appreciate the offer, but we'll have to decline."

"Say *what*?" Lobo said.

"What's wrong with a few days off, sir?" Captain Havoc queried.

"I would like to see the City of Angels," Sparrow Hawk chimed in.

"Forget it," Blade told them.

"May I ask why?" General Gallagher interjected.

"We don't have the time to spare," Blade answered. "You persuaded me to take off for Mexico before I felt the team was ready, and we nearly lost our lives. We need to spend every spare moment in training for when the next assignment comes along."

"Surely you can spare three days," Gallagher prompted.

"No."

"Is that your final word on the subject?"

"Yes."

Lobo snorted. "What a bummer! I was lookin' forward to gettin' me some fresh wool."

Raphaela glanced at the Clansman. "What's fresh wool?"

"Uhhhh—fancy threads," Lobo blurted out.

"Threads?"

"Clothes, Momma. Clothes."

"Oh," Raphaela said. "I could use some new clothes. Will you help me find the right wool?"

Jaguarundi abruptly coughed and turned his back to them, his slim shoulders bouncing up and down.

"What's wrong, brother?" Sparrow asked.

"Listen up," Blade directed sternly. "We're not spending three days in L.A. End of discussion."

General Gallagher pursed his lips and folded his hands behind his back. "There's nothing I could say to change your mind?"

"We need to train," Blade reiterated.

"What if I gave you my word that I won't present another assignment to you for, oh, a month?"

"You can present all the assignments you want. *I* have the final say on whether we accept a mission," Blade reminded him.

"Then why not take advantage of the governor's generous offer?" Gallagher asked. "He's even arranged rooms for all of you at one of the finest hotels in the city. All the food and drinks will be on him."

"I've done died and gone to heaven!" Lobo exclaimed.

"Come on, Blade," the general continued. "Why deprive your people of an honor they deserve? Since you can reject any assignment anyway, simply refuse to go on one until you're satisfied the unit is ready. If Governor Melnick complains, remind him that taking three days off was his idea."

"Please, Blade," Raphaela urged.

"Yeah, give us a break, Jack," Lobo remarked.

"I wouldn't mind getting in some gambling," Doc noted.

The Warrior scrutinized his team for several seconds, his resolve beginning to falter. They had performed well, despite their inexperience. If he denied them their reward, their resentment might create problems later on. At the very least, it would interfere with their training. He looked at the hybrid. "What about you, Jag?"

The mutant swung around. "I'll pass."

"You don't want to go to Los Angeles?"

"I don't like big cities. The humans are always gawking at me."

"Wonder why," Lobo said.

"How would you like your face ripped off?" Jag snapped.

"Oh, yeah? Who's going to do it?"

Jag held his hands out, displaying his inch-long fingernails. "Three guesses."

"You and what army?" Lobo demanded.

"Children! Enough!" Blade barked, glowering and taking a stride toward them.

"Who are you callin' a child?" Lobo inquired resentfully.

The Warrior walked over to the Clansman, towering above the feisty recruit. "*You.*"

Lobo gulped, then smiled. "Well, if you're going to put it that way . . ."

"What's your decision?" General Gallagher inquired.

Blade glanced at Captain Havoc. "Since we're temporarily a democracy, what's your vote?"

The officer shrugged. "Why not? I know L.A. really well, and I wouldn't mind showing the others around."

Annoyed, the Warrior looked at General Gallagher. For someone who had once despised the very idea of a Federation strike team, Gallagher of late was bending over backwards to be nice. Why? Blade wondered. The change of attitude was wonderful, and he knew he shouldn't look a gift horse in the mouth, as it were, but he felt vaguely uneasy about the general's change of heart. Somehow, it rang false.

"So do they get to go or not?" Gallagher queried.

Frowning, Blade responded, "They can go."

Lobo vented a hearty cheer. "Look out, foxes, here comes the lovin' machine!"

"The yo-yo, you mean," Jag quipped.

"Hey, kitty, I'll have you know the ladies can't get enough of me. They fall all over themselves to get a piece of my action."

"Don't call me kitty."

Raphaela stepped forward. "What about you, Blade? Will you be coming to Los Angeles with us?"

"No, thanks."

"Why not?"

"I've been there."

"What's that mean?" Raphaela asked.

"Nothing," Blade said, and nodded at the middle bunker, his HQ. "I've got a lot of paperwork to do. You go and have fun."

"But it won't be the same without you along," Raphaela said sadly, and glanced at the hybrid. "You too, Jag. We're a team, right? We should do things together."

"You have no idea what you're asking," Jaguarundi replied. "If I go to L.A. there will be trouble. Mark my words."

Raphaela looked from the giant to the mutation. "Please. I know this might sound silly, but I've never belonged to a group like this before. Heck, I've never had anyone. My parents died when I was six, and I've pretty much been on my own ever since."

"Who raised you?" Blade inquired, curious about her background. She had been remarkably tight-lipped concerning her past so far, although she had revealed enough to indicate that she had joined the Force to escape an unpleasant situation at the Mound rather than out of any patriotic sense of loyalty to the Federation.

"My aunt," Raphaela divulged, her features downcast. "But she always treated me as an outsider, not one of her own."

"Some folks ain't got no smarts," Lobo remarked.

"And you should know," Jag said.

Raphaela hardly appeared to notice their comments. Her eyes on the ground, she said, "I've never known what it would be like to be part of a regular family. This is the closest I've come, and having all of you as my friends is the greatest thing that's happened to me in ages."

Blade observed an extraordinary reaction in the four men and the hybrid. All five, even the loquacious Clansman, had been hardened by the violence and everyday rigors of the postwar era, yet each one of them seemed to soften as they listened to the Molewoman. Her words struck a responsive chord in the core of their being, and their hearts went out to the innocent waif who so transparently had gotten herself in over her head.

"We're going to be together for a whole year," Raphaela was saying. "We should try and make the most of it. And since our lives will depend on one another, we should stick together as much as possible. We should be just like a family." She paused, gazing at the hybrid. "So, please, Jag. Come with us. For me?"

"But . . ."

"For me?"

Jaguarundi closed his eyes and rubbed his right palm on his sloping forehead. "I know I'll live to regret this, but okay. For you, Raphaela, I'll go to Los Angeles."

"Terrific!" Raphaela declared, and clapped her hands together in delight. "Now what about you, Blade?"

The Warrior shook his head. "Sorry. I can't."

"Please."

"Maybe next time."

"Fuddy-duddy!" Lobo said.

"Well, if Blade can't go, he can't go," General Gallagher stated, his tone implying the giant must be stuck-up. "If the rest of you can be ready by six, I'll have two jeeps here to pick you up."

"We'll be ready, sir," Captain Havoc said.

Gallagher nodded and went to turn, then paused. "Oh. Before I forget. There are two conditions."

Blade glanced at the officer. "Conditions?"

"Yes. We want your people to enjoy themselves, but we also don't want them to attract undue attention. So everyone will wear civvies. No uniforms."

"No problem," Lobo said. "Havoc and the skirt are the only ones who like to wear those overstarched rags anyway."

"Skirt?" Raphaela retorted.

"What's the second condition?" Blade inquired.

"No weapons."

Five seconds of total silence ensued, and then several of the team all tried to talk at the same time.

"No weapons!" Lobo declared. "You must be off your rocker, Miles, baby. There ain't no way old Leo is waltzin' into L.A. without packin' a weapon."

"I don't go anywhere without my Magnum," Doc mentioned.

"And I am not accustomed to traveling unarmed," Sparrow said.

General Gallagher smiled and extended his arms, palms up. "Sorry folks. But there are laws in Los Angeles against carrying weapons. Any weapons. Decades ago, right up to the war, the city had the worst gang problem in the country. The gang members were killing each other off right and left, even mowing down citizens with automatic fire. Laws were passed to stem the tide of weapons," he explained, then added, "Not that such laws ever did any good. Criminals never obtain their weapons through legal channels because the arms are too easy to trace."

"I don't like the idea," Lobo said.

"Take it or leave it. Sorry, but the L.A. authorities take a dim view of anyone caught with a gun or knife. Even though you'll have your special I.D. cards, you could still get in hot water."

"What I.D. cards?" Blade questioned.

"Didn't I tell you? Governor Melnick has authorized the issuance of identification cards specifically for the Force so you can readily identify yourselves anywhere in California, or in any other Federation territory, for that matter."

"Whose idea was this?" the Warrior queried.

"Governor Melnick's."

"An I.D. card is no substitute for an automatic," Lobo noted.

"Those are the terms," General Gallagher said, looking at the Clansman. "What will it be, Lobo?"

"I guess I'll survive three days without my NATO," the Clansman replied reluctantly.

"Doc?"

"I reckon I can do it this once."

"Sparrow?"

"If I want to go with my brothers, I must comply."

"Excellent," Gallagher said, nodding. "Remember, the jeeps will be here for you at six."

"You're all dismissed," Blade instructed them. "Relax and enjoy the rest of the day."

The Force members began to move toward the bunker to the east, their barracks building.

"You know, I'm beginning to like this outfit," Lobo cracked. "All work and no play dampens the old wick, if you get my drift."

Doc Madsen stared at the Clansman. "Don't you *ever* quit flapping your gums?"

Lobo shook his head. "I'm not the shy, quiet type, dude. If I'm walkin', I'm talkin'."

"Tell me about it."

"There is one more thing," General Gallagher said to the Warrior.

"What?"

"I'd like to have a few words with Captain Havoc, if I may?"

"It's a free world," Blade said stiffly, and departed.

General Gallagher smirked and called out, "Captain, might I speak with you a moment?"

The junior officer, already 15 feet away, halted and turned, the corners of his mouth drooping. "Certainly, sir. What about?"

Gallagher motioned for Havoc to approach. "Over here, where we'll have some privacy."

Exhibiting the utmost reluctance, Captain Havoc slung his

M-16 over his right shoulder and walked to within a yard of the general. He stood at attention.

"You can relax, Captain."

"As you wish, sir," Havoc said, and assumed the at-ease stance, his hands clasped in the small of his back.

"Do I detect a note of hostility in your voice?"

"Of course not, sir."

"Then what's bothering you?"

"Nothing, sir."

Gallagher gazed at the retreating Force members to ensure none of them were within hearing range, then growled in a harsh, low inflection, "Don't bullshit me, mister! I know you better than that. Something is eating at you and I want to know what it is right now."

Havoc locked his flinty eyes on the general's. "If you must know, sir, I'm having serious second thoughts."

"About taking revenge for your brother's death?"

"Yes, sir."

"I see," Gallagher said, surprised by the news but not permitting his feelings to show. He pursed his lips and pretended to be interested in a plane flying along the southern horizon, stalling, searching for the right words, not wanting to antagonize Havoc and ruin his best chance ever of permanently disbanding the Force. "I was under the impression you were upset over Jimmy's needless death."

"I was," Havoc admitted, his memory taking him back to that day in October of last year when he had received word of his younger brother's demise. He'd been shocked to discover that Jimmy had perished on an unauthorized mission in Canada, that the Force had been on its way from Alaska to Los Angeles when the pilot of their jet received a distress call on a civilian frequency and Blade decided to land and investigate, even though Canada wasn't even a member of the Freedom Federation.

The Warrior's decision, Havoc believed, had indirectly caused his brother to perish. Sergeant James Havoc, the best noncom in the California military, had given his life to save one of his companions, but the sacrifice seemed senseless in light of the fact that Jimmy's death would never have occurred if Blade had stuck to procedure. If only the Force had flown to L.A. as originally scheduled, Mike Havoc reasoned, his brother would still be alive.

Bitter over the loss, Havoc had listened eagerly to General Gallagher when his superior officer outlined a scheme to get even with Blade for the Warrior's incompetence by gathering proof that the giant was unfit for command. Havoc had agreed to be the general's inside man, to report any slipups Blade made. But on their first mission against El Diablo, despite his resentment and his desire to force the Warrior to step down in disgrace, Havoc had found himself admiring Blade's leadership skills and fearless conduct. Most of all, Havoc had been genuinely moved by the sincere concern Blade displayed for every member of the team. Many times since he had asked himself the same question: Was this a man who would thoughtlessly cause another's death? And the answer that came back every time was a resounding No. He suddenly realized the general was speaking.

"I take it you intend to let Blade off the hook?"

"I don't know."

"You sound confused to me."

"I guess I am, sir."

"Why? Because the last assignment went off without a major hitch? So what? Sooner or later the unit will be out in the field again where Blade's irresponsibility will likely prove fatal for more of you. Five Force members have died already."

"I know."

General Gallagher reached out and placed his right hand on Havoc's arm. "If you don't help me close the Force down, the next death will be on your shoulders."

Havoc's lips compressed into a thin line.

"Listen to me, Captain," Gallagher said. "I've set up the three-day pass to guarantee we accomplish our goal—"

"You set it up, sir?" Havoc interrupted. "I thought you told us Governor Melnick did."

Gallagher grinned craftily. "I persuaded him to do it."

"But why?"

"Don't you see? The new recruits are undisciplined and rowdy. By sending them into L.A. before Blade has finished their training, when they're still thinking more of themselves than the unit as a whole, I'm banking on their inexperience and baser motives to get them into a world of trouble. Let's say, for the sake of argument, that they become drunk and tear up a night spot. How will that look in the press? What will the good people of California think of their precious elite team when some of its members overstep the bounds of propriety? How will Governor Melnick respond when his constituents start clamoring for Blade's head on a platter?" General Gallagher paused and laughed bitterly. "That's where you come in."

"I don't understand, sir. What can I do?"

"It should be obvious. Go along with them. Do whatever you can to turn their three-day pass into a nightmare. Get some of them drunk. Start fights. Let the fools hang themselves. Lobo and Madsen should be easy to dupe considering the short fuse they each possess," Gallagher said. "And there's always Raphaela."

Captain Havoc stood as still as stone, his eyes acquiring a steely gleam the general failed to perceive. "Raphaela, sir?"

"Sure. The bimbo is a babe in the woods. Get her drunk and who knows how big a fool she'll make of herself."

Havoc did not respond.

General Gallagher turned to leave. "Don't let me down, Captain. I'm counting on you.' He smiled, but his next words belied his friendly visage. "And remember, I don't take failure lightly."

CHAPTER THREE

"Check this out! This is my kind of city!"

"How would you know? You've never been to a city like L.A. before."

Lobo, seated across from the California Army trooper who was driving the lead jeep, twisted and looked at Doc Madsen. The Cavalryman sat directly behind him, and next to Madsen was Sparrow Hawk. Havoc, Jag, and Raphaela were riding in the second jeep. "What's with you today, Doc?" Lobo asked. "You've been getting on my case all day."

His eyes on the bright lights of the metropolis through which they were winding, Doc shrugged absently. "Have I?"

"You're mistaken, Lobo," Sparrow added.

"I am?"

The Flathead nodded. "You always seem to think that someone is picking on you, even when they're not. My people have a word for someone like you."

"What is it?" Lobo inquired, expecting to hear one of Sparrow Hawk's sixteen-syllable Indian words.

"Crazy."

L. A. STRIKE

Both Sparrow and Doc burst into laughter.

Sighing, Lobo turned to the driver. "See what I mean? They're always pickin' on me. Pay no attention to them. They're just jealous of my good looks and keen mind."

The trooper, a young corporal who was concentrating on the task of threading through the traffic on the Harbor Freeway, did not even bother to take his gaze from the highway. "If you say so, sir."

"Don't you believe me?"

"I don't *know* you, sir."

"What is this? A conspiracy?" Lobo asked, then added, "And stop callin' me sir."

"I can't, sir."

"Why the hell not?"

"General Gallagher's orders. Every soldier assigned to the Force facility, whether they're guards or drivers or whatever, must always address a Force member as sir," the trooper explained. "Unless, of course, it's the redhead. Her we call ma'am."

"Yeah, I guess old dog-face is a stickler for going by the book, huh?" Lobo commented.

"You don't know the half of it, sir. He's the strictest officer in California."

"Then I'm glad I'm workin' under Blade and not Gallagher," Lobo said. "Blade is a pushover."

The trooper finally glanced at the Clansman. "*Blade*, sir?"

"Yep. I've got him wrapped around my baby pinky."

"The guy who heads the Force? That Blade?"

Lobo nodded.

"The guy who is as big as a frigging mountain and who has more muscles than anyone else on the whole damn planet? *That* Blade?"

"That's the guy. Don't let this get around, soldier, but he's not as tough as he's cracked up to be. Actually, he's a bundle of insecurity."

"I've heard he's the toughest son of a bitch ever to come down the pike," the trooper said, then added, "Sir."

Lobo snorted and shook his head. "Who's been feedin' you that line of bull? Blade's squeeze? I'm tellin' you the guy is a pussycat. He can't make a decision without help. And who do you think he turns to when he's in a bind?"

"Let me guess. You, sir?"

"Damn straight. I'm the real brains behind this outfit."

The trooper shifted and cast a quick glance over his right shoulder at Sparrow Hawk. "I see what you mean, sir."

Riding in the second jeep two hundred feet to the rear, Raphaela stared through the dusty windshield at the first vehicle, then turned to her companions. "What's the matter with you guys? You've hardly spoken a word since we left."

Captain Havoc, seated behind the driver, shrugged. "Sorry. I guess I'm just not in a talkative mood."

Raphaela looked at Jaguarundi. "And what's your excuse?"

The hybrid sat slumped in the seat, his hands folded between his legs. The wind stirred his fur as he gazed morosely at her. "I should never have come along."

"Are you going to start that again?"

"You have no idea what we're in for, Raphaela. Some humans simply do not like mutations. My presence could cause all of you unnecessary aggravation."

"You let us worry about that. I'm happy you came, and I'll bet Mike is too. Aren't you, Captain Havoc?"

The officer appeared not to hear the remark. He was staring off into the distance, his mouth shut tight, his eyes almost blank. Tonight he wore a blue shirt and gray trousers.

"Mike? Did you hear me?"

Havoc blinked three times and faced the Molewoman. "Sorry, Raphaela. What did you say?"

"I said I'm happy Jag came along, and I bet you are also."

"Why wouldn't I be?"

"I should have stayed behind with Blade," Jag stated. "We're in for trouble. I can feel it in my bones."

"You're being silly," Raphaela assured him.

"Am I? You wouldn't say that if you could walk in my footsteps for a day. *You've* never been the target of hatred and bigotry. *You've* never known what it's like to have someone try to kick your face in or put a bullet in your brain simply because you happen to be different. Even in the Civilized Zone, where the people are accustomed to having hybrids in their midst, I still encountered mindless prejudice. Children would stop and stare and point at me. Women would go out of their way to avoid passing me on the street. But the men were the worst. If I were to tell you every insult I've heard, you'd blush for a month."

Raphaela saw the torment etching his countenance and felt a twinge of guilt at convincing him to join them. "You're among friends now. We won't let anyone give you grief."

"What will you do? Beat the crud out of every jerk who looks at me crosswise?"

"Not me," Raphaela said, smiling reassuringly. "Captain Havoc is our martial-arts expert. He holds a black belt in karate, so we'll let him beat the crud out of the jerks."

Jag smiled, despite his misgivings. "You'll have your work cut out for you, Havoc," he said to the officer.

"What?" Havoc replied. Once again he had been gazing into the darkness.

"What's with you, buck-o?" Jag queried. "You're not all here tonight."

"I have a lot on my mind."

"Anything we can help you with?"

Havoc looked at the hybrid for several seconds, his brow furrowed, before responding. "No, but thanks."

"We're like a family now," Raphaela mentioned. "If you have a problem, we'll help out. Any problem. You can always confide in us."

Jag, who sensed that the officer was intensely upset about something, saw the most peculiar expression distort Havoc's features, a strange commingling of melancholy and—what? Anger? At whom? Havoc abruptly swung to the left so they couldn't see his face.

"Thanks, Raphaela."

To change the subject, Jag leaned toward the driver. "How much farther?"

"Not far at all, sir," the trooper dutifully answered. "We'll be at the Bayside Regency in a few minutes."

"What a nice name," Raphaela said. "It sounds elegant."

"It is, ma'am," the trooper confirmed. "You'll be staying at the best hotel in Los Angeles. The Bayside Regency was built about ten years before the war right at the edge of the Royal Palms State Beach. I've never been inside, but I hear the carpet is four inches thick and there's a gold chandelier in the lobby. Real classy joint. They're sparing no expense for you, I can tell you that."

"Wow!" Raphaela stated in amazement. "Governor Melnick and General Gallagher sure are terrific to arrange all this for us."

Jag detected movement out of the corner of his left eye, and he glanced over to see Captain Havoc staring at the Molewoman in undisguised fury. But no sooner did Jag notice than Havoc again swung away. Perplexed, Jag resolved to keep a watchful eye on the officer.

"General Gallagher is a peach," Havoc muttered.

"You've known him for a long time, haven't you?" Raphaela inquired.

"Too long."

"What?"

"Never mind."

Flashing red lights suddenly materialized up ahead. Police cars, an ambulance, and other official vehicles had blocked off the highway, creating a massive traffic jam. Passenger cars and trucks were backed up for hundreds of yards.

"Oh, great," the driver snapped. "Just what we need." He braked and pulled in behind the first jeep. "Looks like we'll be here a while."

"Do you think there was an accident?" Raphaela asked, craning her neck to glimpse the activity near the flashing lights.

"Could be, ma'am," the trooper said. "Who knows? It might be another of those gang shootings."

"Gang shootings?" Raphaela repeated quizzically.

"Yes, ma'am. The newspapers have been filled with the stories. There are two big drug gangs fighting for control of Los Angeles, and they've been killing each other off for over a month now. A lot of innocent bystanders have been killed too."

"Why would they shoot bystanders?"

The driver glanced at her. "Well, ma'am, when there's some idiot speeding down a street at sixty miles an hour and spraying lead all over the place, a lot of folks are liable to be hit."

"Why don't the police put a stop to the gang war?" Jag interjected.

"They try, sir, but there's not a whole hell of a lot they can do other than pick up the pieces. It's not as if the gang members go around advertising who they are, like they did in the old days."

"I don't follow you."

"Well, sir, most of what I'm about to tell you is ancient history, you understand, so I may not get all the facts straight, but before the war the gangs in L.A. would wear their colors to show which gang they belonged to," the soldier detailed.

"Their colors?" Raphaela said.

"Yes, ma'am. Sort of like their uniform. It might be a headband, a bandana, a jacket, or a vest, but it would always be whatever color the gang claimed as their own, or it would have the gang emblem on it."

"And they wore these . . . colors . . . right out in the open?" Raphaela inquired.

"Yes, ma'am, they used to. The gangs before the war had no fear of the law. Hell, in L.A. alone they outnumbered the police by twenty to one. So they paraded around wearing their colors, shooting one another, and dealing drugs. In the process they turned a lot of cities into war zones," the trooper said. "At least, that's what my history teacher in seventh grade taught us."

"And these gangs are still around?"

"Not the same gangs, ma'am. There was a big gang war shortly before World War Three. Two of the gangs, the Bloods and the Crips, came out on top. They wiped out almost all of the others, then went at it themselves. Neither side won, and the gang war weakened both of them. They were easy pickings when the Brothers and the Hollywood Barons came along."

"Who are they?" Raphaela questioned.

"The Brothers and the Hollywood Barons are the gangs that control L.A. today. They were just small gangs once, but they grew like hell after they rubbed out the remainder of the Bloods and the Crips," the trooper said. "Eventually, the Brothers and the Barons took over all of the city. The Brothers have the south side, the Barons the north. And now they're fighting to see which one will be the top dog."

"Do these Brothers and Barons have their own colors?"

"No, ma'am. They gave that up a long time ago. Now the gang members wear tattoos where no one can see them."

"What's a tattoo?" Raphaela queried.

"You don't know what a tattoo is, ma'am?"

"I'm a Mole, remember? We live in seclusion in the Mound. There are a lot of things I know nothing about."

"Well, ma'am, a tattoo is an indelible figure or maybe a mark that a tattooer puts on the body by sticking colored pigment under the skin."

"Sounds painful."

"I wouldn't know, ma'am. I've never had a tattoo put on me."

"What kind of tattoos do the Brothers and the Barons wear?"

"The Brothers wear a tattoo on their left thigh that shows two hands in an overhand shake, a soul grip I think they call it. The Barons wear a tattoo of a crossed dagger and a switchblade under their right arm."

"So the police can't tell who they are unless they take off their clothes," Raphaela said.

"That's the general idea, ma'am."

"I never expected something like this," Raphaela remarked. "The Moles don't have a gang problem."

"You're lucky, ma'am. Do you have drugs at your Mound?"

"Nope. Not unless you count the natural drugs we use for healing purposes."

"There are all kinds of drugs available on the streets of Los Angeles, ma'am. Crack, bennies, acid, meth, coke, mescaline, smack, pot, you name it, the gangs have it. I have two small kids and I sure as hell hope they never become strung out on the stuff."

Raphaela stared at the red lights and frowned. "I never realized it before, but Los Angeles can be a dangerous place to live."

"You've got that straight, ma'am."

"I certainly hope I don't run into any of those horrible gang members."

The soldier chuckled. "I doubt you will, ma'am. There are a lot of decent people living in L.A. too. I didn't mean to get you upset. You don't have a thing to worry about."

CHAPTER FOUR

Fayanne halted under a tree, the darkness enveloping her, and stared at the forbidding estate across the street. Her courage drained to almost nothing, and she clutched the paper bag containing the four blue notebooks to her chest and took a deep breath to steady her nerves.

Don't crap out now!

She licked her lips and scrutinized the massive wall enclosing the four-story mansion, the meticulously maintained yard, and the bright lamps set at 20-foot intervals between the huge front gate and the residence.

Arthur Owsley didn't believe in taking chances.

About to step from the curb, she froze when a match flared to life just inside the gate and a man lit a cigarette.

A guard.

Fayanne knew there would be guards. Lots of them. With the war in full swing, Owsley wasn't about to be careless. He had a reputation for being exceptionally cautious, more prudent, in any event, than Mr. Bad. But then, Owsley didn't have anyone like the Claw in his employ. None of the Holly-

L. A. STRIKE   41

wood Barons possessed a rep like the Claw's. For that matter, no one in the whole damn city was as universally feared as the Claw.

Muffled words arose behind the gate.

Girding herself, Fayanne strode boldly toward the estate, walking as casually as possible. It had taken her 24 hours to muster the spunk to actually deliver the goods. Here was her big chance to even the score and she wanted to relish every moment.

There were three guards stationed at the gate, and they spotted her instantly. One, a tall man in a dark blue suit, stepped up to the iron bars, the cigarette dangling from his thin, cruel lips, and regarded her with a mixture of curiosity and contempt.

"Hello," Fayanne greeted him as she halted a yard from the gate.

"Hello, yourself, foxy," the man replied, raking his eyes up and down her shapely form. "What can we do for you?"

"I'd like to see Mr. Owsley."

The request didn't seem to surprise the guard. "Uh-huh. Now why would a sweet young thing like you want to see the boss?"

"I have something for him."

Smirking, the man stared at a point between her legs and nodded. "I'll just bet you do."

Fayanne struggled to control her rising temper. "It's not what you think."

"Sure, lady," the guard responded sarcastically.

"Really, I have something important for Mr. Owsley."

He glanced at the other two guards and shook his head, then faced her. "Listen, sweet cheeks. We get broads showing up here all the time to see the boss. They all say it's important. And they're all here for the same reason. They all want to hit on the boss."

"But I don't want to hit on him. Honest," Fayanne said, her tone strained, suddenly frightened that her grand scheme might be frustrated by the moron on the other side of the gate.

The man studied her again, noting her faded green blouse and patched jeans, her worn brown shoes, the black purse suspended from her right shoulder, and the brown paper bag in her arms. "Then what do you want?"

"I need to talk to Mr. Owsley."

"Sorry. No."

"Please."

"Take a hike."

Fayanne's anger returned and she stamped her left foot. "Will you at least tell him I'm here?"

"The boss doesn't like to be disturbed unless it's for a good reason."

"Look. I don't know what I can do to convince you I'm here on serious business. Will you call somebody up at the house and have them tell Mr. Owsley that Fayanne Raymond is here? Fayanne Raymond. Got that?"

"Why does that name ring a bell?"

Fayanne stood as straight and proud as she could. "I used to be Mr. Bad's main squeeze."

Startled, the guard did a double take and took a closer scrutiny of her between the bars. "No lie?"

"No lie. And if you don't inform Mr. Oswley, and if he finds out later that I was here, he'll roast your balls over a fire."

"Don't move," the man said, starting toward the left-hand gate post. "And if you're lying to me, bitch, you'll live to regret it."

"I'm not lying."

The guard opened a small cabinet attached to the post and removed a telephone. He spoke into the mouthpiece, then apparently waited for directions from his superiors. A minute later he said a few words, nodded, and replaced the phone.

Fayanne's hopes surged.

"Okay, lady. You're going to get your wish," the man stated as he came back. "I'm to take you up to the house."

Fayanne smiled and clasped the paper bag even tighter. She'd done it! Easy street, here I come! she thought.

The guards promptly unlocked the gate and swung it open, and the tall man beckoned for her to follow him. They headed for the mansion while the other pair locked the gate once again.

"You'd better not be wasting Mr. Owsley's time," the man advised.

"Mister, I'm going to make his day."

The imposing mansion reeked of wealth and luxury. A burly Baron in a three-piece suit admitted them, then dismissed the guard and escorted Fayanne down a tastefully posh corridor to double oak doors at the very end. After rapping twice, he opened the right-hand door and motioned with his left arm. "Go on in."

Suddenly intensely nervous, Fayanne swallowed and moved tentatively past him into a spacious, elegant chamber occupied by four Barons. Three stood at various points in the room. The fourth sat behind a desk the size of a small car, his blue eyes watching her warily.

Arthur Owsley.

The current leader of the Hollywood Barons was an enormous man, as broad as he was tall, heavy but not fat, a great toad of a figure attired in an expensive ebony suit. A bald, round head perched on a squat neck, and his pale pate gleamed in the light as if it had been polished. His thick lips barely moved when he spoke, and yet his voice boomed across the chamber, a low, throaty sound rumbling from his barrel of a chest. "Good evening, Ms. Raymond. Have a seat." He nodded at one of the three chairs arranged in front of his desk.

Fayanne approached slowly, disturbed by the unblinking stare he fixed upon her. "Mr. Owsley," she said. "Thank you for seeing me."

One of the other Barons stepped over to her. "Hold it, sister. I've got to frisk you."

"I'm not packing," Fayanne responded.

Arthur Owsley leaned forward. "Just a formality, Ms. Raymond. I'm certain you understand after having lived with Haywood Keif for several years."

"Yeah, I understand," Fayanne said, extending her arms out, keeping the bag in her right hand. "Go ahead."

The Baron swiftly, expertly, ran his hands over every nook and cranny on her body, then straightened and looked at Owsley. "She's clean, boss." He faced her again. "What's in the bag?"

"A present for Mr. Oswley," Fayanne answered.

"Let me see it."

Fayanne opened the bag so he could view the notebooks, and he stepped aside to permit her to take a seat.

"You have a present for me, Ms. Raymond?" Owsley inquired, his eyes locking onto hers with an almost hypnotic effect.

"Yes, sir. And call me Fayanne, please."

"Very well, Fayanne. You have some explaining to do. Although we have never met before, I recognized your name when the gate guard phoned the house. If my information is correct, you were Mr. Bad's lady for about three years. Correct?"

"Yes."

"And he recently dumped you for Gloria Mundy."

Fayanne's features clouded at the mention of the woman she hated most in the world. She frowned and looked up to find Owsley viewing her intently. "You're very well informed."

A slight smile creased those thick lips. "A man in my position must stay abreast of the latest developments. For the right price, almost any information can be obtained."

"How about the names and addresses of every Brother in the city?"

Owsley finally blinked, his brow knitting as he glanced from the woman to the bag and back again. "That sort of information could not be obtained for any price."

"Until now."

"Do I understand you're here to make a deal?"

"You bet I am," Fayanne stated, expecting Owsley to grab the bag and inspect the contents. Instead, confusing her, he simply sat there.

"Most interesting. But anyone could offer me a list of names, claiming they're the roster of Brothers. Motives, Fayanne, speak louder than words. Why would you want to turn on Mr. Bad?"

"If you know about that bitch Mundy, you shouldn't have

to ask."

Owsley actually smiled. "Revenge? A motive I can relate to very well." He paused and drummed the blunt fingers of his left hand on the desktop. "But you could also have another motive that would have a bearing on your credibility."

"I could?"

"Yes," Owsley said. "You're an addict, Fayanne."

The unexpected assertion caught her off guard. "You're even better informed than I thought."

"I've also heard that Mr. Bad has cut off your credit. No more crack for you unless you can come up with the bread. True?"

Fayanne nodded, amazed at the extent of his knowledge. Owsley's intelligence network of street people and low-level informants in the Brothers appeared to be more efficient than Mr. Bad's. "I know better than to try and hide anything from you, Mr. Owsley. Yeah, the son of a bitch cut off my credit. And after all we meant to each other."

Owsley scrutinized her closely. "For an addict with no source of income, you don't seem to be in need of a fix at the moment."

Fayanne grinned, thinking of the money she had taken from Mr. Bad's safe. "I came into some green recently."

"I see," Owsley said. "What's in the bag?"

"My present for you. Mr. Bad's books."

"His books?"

"He kept them in a safe in his condo. Once a month he'd take them out when the bookkeeper would come over and tally all the receipts and whatnot. Then he'd lock them up again. The bastard doesn't like to have them out of his reach. He doesn't trust anybody, except the Claw, of course."

"Of course." Owsley nodded at one of his men, who promptly brought the bag around the desk.

"You'll find everything you need in there to win your war with the Brothers," Fayanne predicted. "The names and addresses of every Brother, for starters."

Owsley removed the four notebooks and placed them on

the desk. "No one does something for nothing. What do you want in return for these books?"

"Well, I figured you'd be grateful."

"If these prove to be legitimate, I will indeed be grateful," Owsley assured her.

"They're legit, Mr. Owsley. I promise."

The head Baron spread one of the notebooks open and began reading the contents. "You still haven't told me what you want."

Fayanne cleared her throat and shifted in her chair. "Well, I was sort of hoping they'd be valuable."

"Again, if they're genuine, they're quite valuable."

Now that she was on the verge of accomplishing her goal, Fayanne abruptly felt uncomfortable and anxious, wondering if she had done the right thing after all.

"What do you want?" Owsley queried.

"I was sort of hoping you would set me up in style, you know? My own apartment somewhere, a real nice place, not like the dump I'm staying in now. And maybe a little money each month, just enough for me to get by."

Owsley looked at her. "And drugs?"

"Just a little crack now and then, whenever I'm in the need. Unlimited credit. You know," Fayanne said, then added in justification of her request, "It's a pretty fair deal, if you ask me. I'm handing you the Brothers on a silver platter. All I want is what's rightfully mine."

"I see," Owsley said, running his fingers across a page in the notebook. "I'll need to have these books checked by an expert, you understand."

"Sure. No problem."

"How did you happen to come by them?"

Fayanne laughed lightly, beginning to relax, confident of her success. "I pulled one over on that bastard. As you probably know, he keeps his main lady in the condo across from his. I was good enough to bed, but not good enough to live with," she stated spitefully.

"Keif never did have any class," Owsley agreed.

"You've got that straight. Anyway, whenever we were

in his bedroom, which was about every other night or so until he tired of me, I would always try to get a glimpse of the combination on his safe when he opened it."

"Back up a bit. Mr. Bad has the safe in his bedroom?"

"Yep. Hidden behind one of his mirrors."

"And he would open this safe in your presence?"

"Every now and then, whenever he had money or drugs to stick in or take out."

"He trusted you that much?"

"Not really," Fayanne admitted. "Most of the time he'd go into the safe when he thought I was asleep. But I fooled the prick!" She cackled. "I'd pretend to be asleep, then sneak a peek when he worked the combination. And every couple of months I'd get lucky and see one of the numbers clearly. After about two years I had the whole combination."

"Fascinating. But why were you trying to learn the combination when the two of you were still tight?"

Fayanne shrugged. "I don't know. I guess because I resented the fact he didn't trust me completely and wouldn't marry me like I wanted. And it was fun, you know?"

Owsley idly scratched his double chin, then nodded. "Yes, I believe I comprehend the situation fully."

"So do we have a deal?"

"First answer a question for me."

"Anything."

"What does Gloria Mundy look like?"

Surprised, Fayanne's eyes narrowed. What a strange question! What reason could he have for wanting to know about Mundy's appearance? Rather than rock the boat, she said, "The bitch is a redhead. She likes to wear classy threads. Gowns and such."

"What color are her eyes?"

"Her eyes?" Fayanne had to think for a second. "Green, I believe. Yeah. Definitely green."

"Thank you," Owsley said. "And now to the matter of these notebooks."

"Yes?" Fayanne said eagerly.

"When did you appropriate them?"

"Yesterday."

"Hmmmm," Owsley said. "So Mr. Bad has been aware of their absence for a whole day?"

"No," Fayanne replied. "Like I told you, he usually only takes the books out of the safe when his accountant enters all the receipts and stuff. Once a month, like clockwork, and the next time won't be for a couple of weeks yet."

"Perhaps he only *uses* the books once a month, but you just admitted that he goes into the safe every other night or so to deposit or take out drugs and money. Correct?"

"Yeah. But—" Fayanne began.

"Then don't insult my intelligence again," Owsley said sternly. "Do you think I was born yesterday? Mr. Bad is my worst enemy, but I'll be the first to admit he's no dummy. If he opens his safe to stash some dope, don't you think he's bound to notice a little thing like his notebooks being missing?"

"Yes," Fayanne admitted sheepishly. "But if you act fast, you can still catch the Brothers off guard."

"Perhaps. But if Mr. Bad has had twelve hours or more in which to warn them, my people will end up walking into a trap. No, I'm afraid that the time differential diminishes the value of the notebooks somewhat."

Forgetting herself, angered at the thought she might not receive as much as she had hoped, Fayanne leaned forward. "What the hell are you trying to pull, mister? A couple of minutes ago you were saying the notebooks are quite valuable."

"They are."

"Good," Fayanne said, relieved.

"But not as valuable as you hope."

"I can't believe this!" Fayanne snapped. "I risked my ass to bring those lousy books to you, and you're dumping on me!"

"My dear Ms. Raymond, had you given me fair warning the notebooks were going to be delivered, I would have arranged to meet you ten minutes after you made the snatch. That way my boys could have wiped out two-thirds of the

Brothers before those bastards knew what hit them."

"You can still wipe them out," Fayanne stated.

"It is unlikely. The odds are that Mr. Bad has alerted his underlings by now and they will be waiting for the Barons to invade their turf."

"I've got an idea," Fayanne mentioned. "Why don't you turn the notebooks over to the police. Let the police finish them off."

"Out of the question."

"Why?" Fayanne wanted to know.

"Because the war is strictly between the Barons and the Brothers. Neither of us will involve outside parties, least of all the police."

"You're blowing a great opportunity," Fayanne commented.

Owsley's mouth compressed and he glared at her. "Don't presume to sit in judgment on me, bitch. Your minuscule mind can't possibly comprehend the factors I must take into consideration to reach a decision on a matter like this."

Afraid she had antagonized her sole hope of obtaining crack, Fayanne abruptly acquiesced. "Okay. I'm sorry. Don't get your gums in an uproar." She paused. "So what's the bottom line? Give it to me straight."

"I have no intention of setting you up for life in an apartment when you're perfectly capable of finding and paying for your own."

Fayanne slumped in her chair, dejected.

"Nor will I extend unlimited credit to you so you can indulge in an orgy of drug-taking. No one qualifies for unlimited credit."

Monumentally depressed, Fayanne stared at the floor. "No apartment. No drugs. What *do* I get? A pack of chewing gum?"

"Even if the Brothers have been forewarned, knowing all of their names is an advantage that will enable us to win this war in the end," Owsley said, folding his hands on the desk. "Therefore, I'm prepared to pay you a fair price for the notebooks and an added bonus in recognition of your service to the Barons."

Fayanne perked up. "How fair is fair?"

"I was thinking in the neighborhood of three hundred thousand dollars."

For several seconds Fayanne simply sat there, stunned, speechless, her drug-benumbed mind in neutral. Finally she blinked several times and said in a whisper, "Three hundred thousand dollars?"

"Correct. Do you agree that the figure is an equitable sum?"

"Mr. Owsley, you're the fairest man who ever lived."

The leader of the Hollywood Barons smiled and nodded at one of his men. "J.J. here will see to it that you receive the funds. Would you prefer cash or a certified check?"

"Cash," Fayanne blurted out. "Definitely cash."

Owsley nodded. "Then that will be all."

"Thank you, sir," Fayanne said, rising and backing toward the doors. "Thank you, thank you, thank you."

"Spend your riches wisely."

"Oh, I will, Mr. Owsley. You don't have to worry about me none," Fayanne promised. She turned and exited as the Baron named J.J. held the door for her.

Arthur Owsley leaned back, watching her depart with a delighted grin creasing his countenance. He glanced at a nearby Baron. "Ahhhh, the grand irony of life. Wouldn't you agree, Barney?"

"Boss?"

"To think that that miserable bitch has handed us victory on a silver platter!"

"She has?"

"Most assuredly."

"Because now we know the names of the Brothers, huh?"

"Knowledge is only half the battle, Barney. It's how you use your knowledge that counts," Owsley philosophized. "For instance, in this particular case we are going to use our knowledge to its maximum advantage."

"How, Boss?"

"By announcing to the entire world that we have the

notebooks."

"Huh?"

Owsley stared at his stocky lieutenant. "Give the word. I want every dealer in our organization to tell every client, every hooker, every snitch on the street that we've purchased Mr. Bad's books from Fayanne Raymond for three hundred thousand dollars."

"Let me get this straight. You *want* everybody to know?"

"You'll never have to worry about someone accusing you of having a rapier wit," Owsley said dryly. "Yes, I want everybody to know."

"But why, Boss?"

"Because once the rank and file in the Brothers discover we know their identities, they'll do some serious soul-searching. Many of them might decide to turn over, especially when they learn Mr. Bad's own ex-squeeze dumped on him."

Barney digested the information for a minute. "But what good will it do if Mr. Bad has already warned them you have the books?"

"Hearing the news from their boss is one thing. Hearing the news bandied about on the street, with our people bragging to every mother's son about how we pulled a fast one on the Brothers, is bound to have an effect on their morale. This is the coup of the decade. The lower-rank Brothers will begin to wonder about Mr. Bad's leadership. They'll wonder if he can cut it any more. Combine the news of the books with the little surprise we have in store for Mr. Bad, and his days as head of the Brothers are numbered."

"You're a genius, Boss," Barney said in appreciation.

Owsley nodded. "I know. Now start spreading the word."

"Right away," Barney replied, and took several strides. A thought occurred to him and he halted and turned. "Say, Boss?"

"What is it *now*, Barney?"

"If we go spreading the news all over the street, then Mr. Bad will know who swiped his notebooks. That Raymond dame's life won't be worth a plugged nickel."

A cackle erupted from Owsley's lips and his massive body shook and quivered. "I know," he declared. "Ain't life a bitch?"

CHAPTER FIVE

"Wow! Ain't this joint bitchin'?" Lobo asked in astonishment, gaping at the golden chandelier suspended 40 feet above the enormous lobby.

"It looks like the Taj Mahal," Captain Havoc commented.

Lobo glanced at the officer. "The who?"

"Never mind."

"Let's check in," Doc Madsen suggested.

The six Force members moved slowly from the entrance of the Bayside Regency toward the ornate front desk, drawing astounded stares from the patrons of the posh establishment.

"Why is everyone lookin' at us?" Lobo wondered.

"It must be my buckskins," Sparrow said. "I haven't seen one person wearing buckskins since we entered the city."

Doc reached up and tilted his wide-brimmed hat back on his head. "Beats me what the dickens they're gazing at. Some folks don't have any manners."

Jaguarundi, who was at the center of their small group, sighed. "It's me. I warned you this would happen. Most humans get all bent out of shape at the mere sight of a hybrid like me."

They were passing a cluster of chairs where several expensively dressed men and women sat, gawking at the new arrivals. One lady, who weighed approximately 220 pounds, frowned and shook her head.

"What's your problem, fatso?" Lobo demanded.

His remark caused the woman's mouth to go slack and she pressed her right hand to her bosom. "Well, I never!"

"Don't come cryin' to me," Lobo responded. "I wouldn't touch your fat buns with a ten-foot pole."

The woman appeared about to have a conniption. Her mouth opened and closed repeatedly, resembling a fish out of water. "You . . . you uncouth person!"

"Oh, yeah?" Lobo retorted. "I can be as couth as the next clown, sister."

"Don't, Lobo," Raphaela said.

"Why not? The bimbo started it."

"Please. We should be on our best behavior."

"I *am* behavin' myself," the Clansman replied testily.

Raphaela smiled warmly at the heavyset woman, hoping to offset Lobo's crude comments with a little friendliness, but the woman only turned up her nose and averted her gaze. Oh, well. She'd tried. She looked down at her plain brown shirt and black pants, the only other set of clothes she owned besides her fatigues, and then at the beautiful dresses being worn by the clientele of the hotel, and felt self-conscious of her shabby apparel.

"Hey, Havoc?" Lobo said as they neared the front desk.

"What is it?"

"What the hell does uncouth mean?"

The captain, who had roused himself from his moodiness in the jeep, regarded the Clansman for a moment. "Do you ever pick your nose in public?"

"Sure. Doesn't everybody?"

"Then you're uncouth."

"Oh. So it *ain't* an insult?"

A white-haired man in an immaculate black tuxedo watched them approach, the corners of his mouth curved downward, scrutinizing them with the air of a man inspecting a can of putrid garbage. "May I assist you people?" he asked scornfully.

"Damn straight, Jack," Lobo replied cheerily. "Where's our rooms?"

The man straightened and placed his neatly filed fingers on the top of the polished desk. "I beg your pardon?"

"Didn't you hear the man?" Doc queried. "We want our rooms."

"You people intend to stay *here*?"

Lobo snorted. "No. We just came by to ask your permission to jack off in your lobby."

"Lobo!" Raphaela stated sternly.

"This guy's a dork."

Captain Havoc stepped to the counter and smiled wanly. "Sorry about the Neanderthal. My name is Mike Havoc." He gestured at his companions. "We were sent by General Gallagher. I understand you have reservations for us."

"Havoc?" the desk clerk said, then did a double take. "*You* people are the Force?"

"That's us, chuckles," Lobo confirmed. "In the gorgeous, ever-lovin' flesh."

"Are you *sure* you're the Force?"

Doc Madsen leaned on the counter. "Was that a joke of some kind, mister?"

"No. No. Of course not," the man replied. "I've read about your exploits in the paper, but I never expected you to look . . . like . . . you do."

Lobo puffed out his chest. "Yeah. I know what you mean, dude. Wait until the babes get a load of this bod."

"What?"

"Ignore him," Havoc suggested. "What about our rooms?"

Clearing his throat, the desk clerk pivoted and extracted two keys from the cubbyholes behind the registration desk. "Rooms, sir? You have better than mere rooms. Both the Presidential Suite and the Ambassador Suite on the top floor have been reserved exclusively for all of you." He faced them and handed the keys to Havoc. "Each executive suite contains three separate bedrooms," he detailed, and smiled at Raphaela. "You will have all the privacy you require."

"Thank you," the Molewoman replied gratefully.

"Do you have any bags?" the desk clerk inquired.

"I have a paper bag I use for collecting herbs at our facility," Sparrow Hawk mentioned. "But I didn't bring it with me."

"No, sir. I meant do you have any luggage?"

"Lug what?" Lobo responded.

"No luggage," Havoc said.

For the first time the desk clerk appeared to notice Jaguarundi. "Is this . . . gentleman . . . with you?"

"He is," Havoc stated.

"Does he require any special facilities?"

"Like what, partner?" Doc rejoined.

The man studied the hybrid's fur and loincloth, then the mutant's feline features, his brow knit in perplexity. "The Bayside Regency prides itself on being able to satisfy the needs of every guest. Should we send out for some kitty litter?"

For a moment no one moved or spoke, and then Jaguarundi lunged, his tapered nails sweeping up, his mouth twisted in a snarl. "Kitty litter!"

Fortunately for the terrified desk clerk, Captain Havoc and Doc Madsen intervened, each man grabbing one of the hybrid's arms and holding tight.

"Let me at him!" Jag snarled, his indignation aroused, struggling to break free. "I'll rip him to shreds!"

"Calm down!" Havoc stated. "He didn't mean anything by it."

White as the shirt he wore, the man behind the desk had backed up against the cubbyholes, his left hand to his throat. "I'm sorry!" he blurted out. "I never intended to offend you."

"Come on, Jag," Doc urged, restraining the hybrid with difficulty. "Let it ride."

"Yeah, dude. Chill out," Lobo interjected. "How's this dummy supposed to know you've been house trained?"

Jag's enraged visage swung toward the Clansman. "*House trained!*" he bellowed, and lunged again, only this time at

Lobo, his nails coming within an inch of the Clansman's chest.

"Hey! What did I say?" Lobo snapped, retreating a good yard.

Captain Havoc glanced at the former gang member. "Nice going, rocks-for-brains."

"What the hell did I do?" Lobo demanded angrily.

The desk clerk looked at Raphaela, who had stepped to one side and was watching the proceedings in an attitude of resigned despair. "I say, miss, are your friends always so . . . temperamental?"

"No," Raphaela replied, smiling sweetly.

"Thank goodness."

"This is one of their calmer moments."

"I wish Blade was here," Sparrow Hawk commented. "This promises to be a long three days."

Jaguarundi was still trying to get at Lobo, who now added insult to injury by sticking his thumbs in his ears and waggling his fingers while sticking out his tongue. "Let go of me!" Jag cried. "He has this coming!"

Captain Havoc and Doc Madsen were holding on for dear life.

Just then, as the desk clerk was reaching for the telephone to call the police, Raphaela walked over to the hybrid and gently rested her right hand on his shoulder. "Enough, Jag," she said softly.

Jag looked at her, his features contorted in fury. "You can't be serious! Didn't you hear him?"

"Enough," Raphaela repeated quietly.

To everyone's astonishment, the hybrid slowly relaxed, his anger subsiding, and his arms dropped to his sides.

Raphaela turned to the Clansman. "Apologize, Lobo."

"Say what?"

"Apologize to Jag."

"Why should I apologize? He's the one who can't control his temper," Lobo said defensively.

"Apologize," Raphaela reiterated firmly.

Lobo muttered a few words under his breath, then glanced at the hybrid. "Sorry," he mumbled.

"Say it louder," Raphaela directed.

"What for? He heard me."

"Please."

The Clansman puckered his lips and sighed. "All right. You can't say I don't have any class. Sorry, Jag. I didn't mean to get you ticked off."

Jag averted his gaze, his head bowed, embarrassed by his rowdy display. "I'm sorry too. I'm just a bit touchy about my condition."

"A bit?" Lobo said, and snorted. "Why, if—"

"Lobo!" Raphaela stated.

"Sorry, gorgeous."

Raphaela faced the front desk. "My apologies for our behavior. I'm afraid our excitement at being in Los Angeles has all of us on edge."

The desk clerk coughed and eased tentatively to the edge of the counter, his eyes warily watching Jag. "Is this your first time to the city?"

"Yes."

"Then you'll undoubtedly be celebrating by going out on the town."

"Maybe," Raphaela answered, glancing uncertainly at her companions.

"Perhaps I could offer a suggestion?" the desk clerk said kindly.

"By all means."

"Our staff was instructed to accord you every courtesy. Anything you want is yours, and the governor's office is picking up the tab. If you plan to celebrate, you should be dressed accordingly. Right around the corner from the Regency, to the east, is an outstanding clothing store. Only the finest fashions. I know the manager well, and I would be delighted to give her a call and inform her you're coming over. What do you say?"

"I don't know," Raphaela replied. "No one told us the governor would buy us new clothes."

"I don't need new duds," Doc remarked. "These are good for another six months easy."

"And I prefer my buckskins," Sparrow said.

"Well, *I* could use some new leather," Lobo declared.

"Leather?" the desk clerk said distastefully. "I'm not quite sure if The Sophisticate sells leather clothing."

"How good can the store be if they don't sell leather, man?" Lobo responded. "Leather is bitchin'."

"Bitchin'?"

Raphaela glanced at Havoc. "What do you think? Should we buy clothes and have the governor pay for them? Will General Gallagher be mad at us?"

A peculiar smile flitted across the officer's face. "Why not?" If the governor gets upset, General Gallagher can always pay for the clothes himself."

"I guess it would be okay," Raphaela told the desk clerk.

"Wonderful. My name is Seymour, by the way. If there's anything I can do for you, you have just to say the word," he said, and gave her his most charming smile.

Lobo snickered. "Seymour? I should've known."

"Let's go up and check out our suites," Havoc suggested, jangling the keys. "Then we'll see about buying new clothes for Raphaela."

The Molewoman blinked. "Me? What about you? I'm not going to be the only one who buys clothes."

"Enjoy your stay at the Regency," Seymour said pleasantly.

"Where are the stairs?" Raphaela inquired, scanning the lobby.

"Stairs? My dear lady, the executive suites are on the twentieth floor," Seymour informed her. "You can take one of the elevators."

"What's an elevator?"

Seymour stared at her intently for several seconds, apparently trying to determine if she was serious. "If you don't mind my asking, where *are* you from?"

"Let's go," Havoc stated, and led the way toward the elevators positioned along the west wall.

"So where should we go after we got the threads?" Lobo asked of no one in particular.

"I'm not going anywhere," Jag said.

"Do you plan to spend all three days in your bedroom,

brother?'' Sparrow inquired.

"Now there's an idea."

They reached the elevators and the officer pressed the UP button. Seconds later an elevator to their right opened with a muted hiss.

"All aboard," Havoc said, and gestured for them to enter.

"I've never been in an elevator before," Raphaela mentioned as she stepped inside. "What does it do?"

"I don't know," Sparrow answered, joining her. "I have never been in one either."

They piled in and Havoc pushed the appropriate button for the twentieth floor.

"Thank goodness we have you along, Mike," Raphaela declared, and touched his arm. "We'd be lost without you."

Havoc glanced at her, then stared at the floor indicator. "What are friends for?" he replied, a bit gruffly.

"We're rising," Sparrow said.

Raphaela stood still, astounded by the sensation of floating skyward, her skin tingling, thrilled by the new experience. "Elevators are neat."

"What a bunch of chumps," Lobo cracked.

"I suppose you've ridden in an elevator before?" Doc asked him.

"Well, I never exactly rode in one. But I saw 'em in the Twin Cities and an old-timer told me what they were used for," Lobo disclosed.

In short order the elevator arrived and the door opened to reveal a luxurious corridor.

"Everybody out," Havoc stated. He walked along the hall until he came to the door marked PRESIDENTIAL SUITE and inserted the key.

"Do you think these digs come with free eats?" Lobo asked. "I'm gettin' hungry."

"You're always hungry," Doc noted.

"I'm a growin' boy."

"At least from the neck down," Jag added.

Grinning, Havoc thrust the door wide open and strode into a gigantic chamber large enough to accommodate 50 people, furnished opulently, a fitting domicile for the richest of the rich. The green carpet felt spongy underfoot.

"Goodness gracious!" Raphaela declared as she gaped at the lavishly adorned suite. "This is magnificent."

"It's no big deal," Lobo said. "I'm going to have a place one day that'll make this joint look like a cave."

"Dream on," Jag said.

They fanned out, inspecting the various rooms, except for Havoc, who stood by the door watching them, grinning in amusement.

Raphaela, Sparrow, and Lobo came to the immense bathroom and gazed at the shining tiled floor and the sparkling facilities.

"Our barracks should be this clean," Lobo quipped.

Sparrow stared at the toilet, then at a strange, bowl-shaped fixture nearby that resembled the toilet in size but lacked a seat and a flush tank. "What is this?" he inquired.

"I don't know," Raphaela admitted, shaking her head. "I've never seen anything like it."

"Maybe it's a toilet they never finished," Sparrow speculated.

"Boy, are you guys dumb," Lobo said.

"Do you know what this is?" Raphaela asked.

"Of course. *Some* of us aren't from the sticks, you know."

"Then what is it?" Sparrow queried.

"It's a bathtub for babies."

CHAPTER SIX

Seymour heard their voices and pivoted, tensing at the prospect of dealing with the barbarians again, and he spied the group coming through the front doors. There was the cowboy in black and the short Indian in buckskins, the loudmouth in the black leather jacket, and the somber, dignified blond man who appeared capable of tearing the L.A. phone book in half with his bare hands. He peered at the other two, and it took him several seconds to recognize them. "Good Lord!" he breathed in astonishment.

The redhead was stunning. She had on a form-fitting blue gown, and the fabric glistened in the light, casting her body in a shimmering aura. The bottom hem almost brushed against the carpet. Her shoulders were bare, and the snug material covering her bust accented her ample cleavage. Over her left shoulder hung a new purse. Evidently self-conscious of her appearance, she walked with her head down.

Even more surprising was the last member of the team. He wore a new black pinstriped suit and a spiffy fedora. A casual glance would not reveal anything out of the ordinary except for the brown sandals he wore instead of shoes. But closeup there would be no mistaking the fur and the feline features.

"I see you took my advice," Seymour stated as they neared the registration desk.

"Some advice," Lobo responded. "The bimbo didn't even have any leather pants. Pitiful."

"What do you think of my dress?" Raphaela inquired innocently, and spun in a circle.

"My dear, you look positively sensational," Seymour assured her. He wondered why her shoes seemed to bulge the bottom of her gown.

"We're fixin' to do some heavy partyin'," Lobo said. "Where's a really hot spot?"

"What type of entertainment do you prefer?"

"Topless broads."

"We're not taking Raphaela to a topless bar," Doc Madsen declared.

"Why not?" Lobo replied. "The broads won't have anything she hasn't seen before."

"Raphaela is a lady," Sparrow said. "To take her to such a place would be an insult."

"Why?" the Clansman asked.

"We want somewhere quiet and peaceful," Jaguarundi stated. "Somewhere we won't be noticed."

Lobo glanced at the hybrid. "No one will notice you in that getup."

Raphaela came to the counter. "Will you help us, Seymour? Mike was supposed to show us the town, but he's leaving it up to us."

"I don't know which nightclub to recommend," Seymour said. "You're such a diverse group."

"There's nothin' different about us," Lobo snapped.

Seymour brightened as an idea occurred to him. "There is one particular club that quite a few of our younger guests frequent, and the cuisine and floor shows have received favorable reviews in the press."

"What's the name of this joint?" Lobo asked.

"The China White."

"Is it far?" Raphaela inquired. "I don't want to do a lot of walking in this gown. To tell you the truth, I'm almost afraid to *sit down* in it."

Seymour grinned. "You can take a cab to the China White. The nightclub is in Long Beach, off Ocean Boulevard. Not very far at all."

"Is it expensive?" Doc queried.

"It is a high-class establishment, yes."

"Just our style," Lobo declared.

Captain Havoc tapped on the counter to get their attention, and when they all gazed at him, said, "I hate to be a spoilsport, but we'll need a lot of money to have a good time at this place. They don't pass out drinks for free. I have about seventy-five dollars. How are you fixed?"

"All I have is the money I've saved from our subsistence allowance," Raphaela said, referring to the monthly stipend paid to the Force members by the governor's office. Since their food, clothing, and shelter were already provided, they only received one hundred dollars in California currency every four weeks. "About sixty dollars."

"That should be enough," Lobo said, not bothering to mention he had eighty dollars on him. "How much can they charge for a drink at this fancy place, anyway?"

Seymour coughed. "I believe the going price is fifteen dollars."

"For one lousy drink? You've jivin' us, old-timer."

"He's serious," Havoc confirmed. "And there will be a cover charge to get in the door."

"Forty dollars per person," Seymour said.

"Forty bucks?" Lobo sputtered. "Let's forget the China White and find a place with topless chicks."

"Where did you hear about these topless women?" Doc inquired.

"From one of the California Army guards out at our headquarters," Lobo disclosed. "He told me about this bitchin' bar called the Rat's Nest where—"

"The Rat's Nest?" Doc repeated.

"Yeah. Doesn't it sound terrific?"

Sparrow leaned toward the Clansman. "No."

"Is that your final answer?" Lobo asked.

"Let me put it this way," the Flathead said. "How do you feel about being scalped?"

"I would be more than happy to call the China White and explain the situation to the management there," Seymour proposed. "I'm certain they'll permit you to ring up a tab and the governor's office will pay the bill."

"I've already spent too much money on this gown," Raphaela said. "I don't want to spend any more."

"What's the use of new threads if you can't show them off?" Lobo commented. "I vote we go check out this dive."

"For once I agree with Lobo," Doc said. "What harm can it do?"

"I have never been to a nightclub," Sparrow added. "I would like to go."

Raphaela looked at Captain Havoc. "What about you, Mike? Do you want to go?"

"If all of you are going, I wouldn't miss it for the world."

"Well, you'd better keep an eye on us," Raphaela advised. "None of us have ever been to a ritzy nightclub. We don't want to embarrass ourselves or do anything that might reflect badly on the Force, so we'll rely on you to guide us along."

Havoc stared at her for several seconds before replying. "No problem."

"Then it's settled! Let's boogie," Lobo said.

"Thank you for your help, Seymour," Raphaela remarked.

"My pleasure, madam," the desk clerk responded politely. "The doorman knows all about you. Tell him I said to hail you a cab. He'll know what to do."

"Thanks, again."

"Any time," Seymour responded, watching them walk toward the entrance and musing that during his long and illustrous career in the hotel industry he had never beheld such an outlandish group. He felt profound sympathy for the lovely redhead, thrust in as she was among such crude primitives. All except for the blond man, the officer named

Havoc. Now *he* appeared to be a perfect gentleman and the only reliable one in the bunch.

Sighing, Seymour checked in the phone book for the number of the China White and dialed. When a woman answered, he asked to speak with the manager. After a minute a gruff voice came on the line.

"Yeah? Who is it?"

"Is this the manager?"

"No, he's busy. Can I help you?"

"I was hoping to speak directly to the manager," Seymour stated. "This is very important."

"I told you he's busy."

"Very well. Will you relay a message to him for me?"

"Who are you?"

"Seymour Parkfeld, at the Bayside Regency. To whom am I speaking?"

"The name is Claw."

"My, what an unusual name."

"What's the message, man? I don't have all night."

"Well, it's like this," Seymour said, and went into full detail about the Force and their three-day pass and the unlimited credit extended by the governor's office. He concluded with, "They are on their way over to the China White right this moment. If you would be so kind, simply tally their bill at the end of the night and let me know. The governor's office will promptly issue you a check."

"Let me get this straight, man. You want me to extend credit to these Force types?"

"That's it in a nutshell."

"*You're* the one who's nuts, Seymour, baby, if you expect my boss to give credit to these turkeys. I don't know them."

"Don't you read the papers?"

"No."

"But they're the *Force*. Their credit is good."

"Not with us it ain't."

"You're being terribly rude," Seymour mentioned. "I insist on speaking to the manager."

"Insist this," the other man said, and a second later the

dial tone filled the receiver.

"My word," Seymour said to himself. He gazed out the glass doors, hoping to find the Force still there, but they were already gone. "Oh, my," he mumbled, and hung up. *Now* what should he do? The Force would show up at the China White, probably tally a huge bill, and have no way of paying their tab. He pressed his right hand to his cheek.

"Oh, *my!*"

They piled out of the taxi and stood gaping at the bright neon lights dominating the roof of the China White. The club was three stories high and painted a vivid chartreuse. Cars were constantly coming and going, and a steady stream of customers entered and departed, most laughing and engaged in lively banter.

"That'll be twelve bucks," the cab driver announced, extending his right arm toward them.

Lobo leaned down and peered in the open passage-side window. "Hey, dude, are you askin' us for money?"

"No, I'm asking for your autograph," the cabbie replied sarcastically. "Of course I want my money, you moron."

"Hey, aren't you hip to the facts, mister?"

"What facts are you talking about?"

Raphaela joined the Clansman by the window. "Didn't the doorperson tell you?"

"You mean the doorman at the Regency?"

"Yes."

"What was he supposed to tell me? That you're all deadbeats?"

"No," Raphaela said, smiling. "He was supposed to let you know that the governor is paying for all our bills."

The cabbie, a portly man in his forties, did a double take. "The governor?"

"Yes. Governor Melnick. He runs California. Have you heard of him?"

"Who hasn't, lady?"

"Good. Then all you have to do is call him and he'll make sure you get your money."

"You want me to call the *governor*?"

Raphaela nodded.

"How about if I call the cops instead?"

"The cops?"

"Yeah, lady. The L.A.P.D. They can toss you in a cell and throw away the key for all I care."

Puzzled by the cab driver's reaction, Raphaela was about to try and convince him of her sincerity when Captain Havoc materialized at her right elbow.

"How much do we owe you?" the officer inquired.

"Twelve bucks. Unless, of course, you'd like to call Santa Claus and get the money from him."

"Who is Santa Claus?" Raphaela queried. "A friend of the governor's?"

"Is she for real?" the cabbie asked Havoc.

The captain ignored the question and withdrew his wallet from his right rear pocket. He fished out twelve dollars and reached inside. "Here."

"Thanks," the cabbie said, snatching the bills as if he was afraid the fare would change his mind.

Raphaela straightened. "Well, let's go in and have some fun."

The cabbie saw them start up the cement steps to the nightclub. He leaned toward the window and motioned at the blond guy, who had started to turn away.

Havoc swung around. "What is it?"

"You can level with me."

"Level?"

"Yeah. Give it to me straight. Are the people you're with from a looney bin?"

"No."

"Come on. Then they must be a theater group, right?"

"Nope."

"But that guy with all the facial hair. Where'd you dredge him up at?"

Havoc pointed at Raphaela. "He's her husband."

The cabbie glanced at the furry man in the fedora, then at the radiant redhead. "Yuck. That's gross. What does she see in an animal like him?"

Struggling to keep a straight face, Havoc looked at his teammates to ensure they were too far away to hear his next remark, then eased a little farther into the window. "Don't tell anyone," he whispered.

"Yeah? Yeah?"

"She's a nympho, and he's got a pecker fifteen inches long."

The cab driver's mouth fell open.

Smirking, Havoc turned and caught up with the others. They were waiting for him just outside the door. All of them were staring at him expectantly, relying on him to lead them, and a twinge of guilt racked him at the thought of General Gallagher's instructions.

"What was that all about?" Jag queried, nodding at the taxi.

"He finally realized who we are and apologized for giving Raphaela such a hard time," Havoc fibbed.

"What a nice man," the Molewoman said. She gazed at the nightclub apprehensively. "Shall we go in?"

"Allow me," Havoc said, and opend the door for them. His eyes narrowed at the sight of two tall, lean men standing a few feet away. They were studying everyone who entered and left the China White. One was black, the other white, yet they wore identical brown suits and identical hairstyles. Under the left arm of each, noticeable only to a professional like Havoc, was the telltale bulge of a gun in a shoulder holster.

"Hold it," the black declared as they entered.

"Hey, bro! What's happenin'?" Lobo greeted him.

"Don't bro *me*, geek. I've never seen you people here before," the man stated.

"This is our first time," Raphaela told him. "We hear this is a hot spot."

"Are you from out of town?"

"Yes," Havoc answered before any of his companions could reply. "We're staying at the Bayside Regency and the desk clerk recommended this place."

The black and the white looked at one another.

"The Regency, huh?" the white one said. "You have to be loaded to stay there."

"We're stayin' in the executive suites," Lobo bragged.

"Is that a fact?" the black responded. "Well, then, let me welcome you to the club. The cover charge will be added to your bill. Anything you want, you can have. Anything." He emphasized the last word meaningfully.

"Thank you," Raphaela said. "People in Los Angeles certainly are considerate."

"We aim to please, lady," the black said. "My name is Dexter. My friend here is Sheba. We're the bouncers. If anyone gives you any grief, you tell us."

"Sheba?" Lobo said, and cackled. "What a name for a guy."

The white bouncer scowled and took a half step toward the Clansman. "And what's your name, buster?"

"Lobo."

"Like you have room to talk."

Havoc saw Lobo bristle and open his mouth, and he quickly gave the Clansman a shove, sending him along the wide hallway leading to the club floor. "Don't mind him. He's had a little too much to drink."

"Make damn sure he behaves himself," Dexter advised.

"We will," Havoc responded cheerily, and gave a friendly wave as he started forward. What sort of club was this? he wondered. Why were armed guards stationed at the entrance? Did Dexter's comment about anything being available mean what he thought it meant? An uneasy feeling arose within him and he scanned his teammates. "You know, maybe coming here wasn't such a bright idea. Why don't we return to the Regency and order in some pizza?"

"We've come this far," Doc noted. "Why go back now?"

"I can hear music," Sparrow mentioned.

Jaguarundi gazed around at the dark shadows, then at the dim overhead lights. "This place isn't too bad. At least no one will notice me."

"I'd like to stay," Raphaela said.

"Suit yourselves," Havoc told them, and frowned, his inexplicable anxiety mounting by degrees with every stride he took.

"Don't worry, Mike," Raphaela said. "We'll be on our best behavior. What could go wrong?"

CHAPTER SEVEN

He'd done the wrong thing.

Blade leaned back in his chair and stared at the mountain of paperwork on the desk in front of him. When he'd accepted the offer to head the Force, he'd had no idea there would be so much pencil-pushing involved. Or pen-pushing. Whatever. It seemed as if seldom did a day go by that a report wasn't required to be filed. Personnel reports. Performance critiques. Supply requisitions. And on and on it went. A never-ending stream of paper flowing from his desk to the governor's office, by way of General Gallagher, of course.

Gallagher.

The Warrior stretched, thinking that the general had been behaving strangely of late. Why? Every time he mentioned Athena Morris, Gallagher almost laid an egg. Was the general extremely upset about her death, or was there another reason? And what was going on between Gallagher and Captain Havoc? The pair had been conducting a lot of private, almost secretive conversations recently.

Blade thought of the Force members and placed his hands

on the desktop. He'd done the wrong thing, undoubtedly. He should have gone with them to Los Angeles. They were *his* people, damn it, and they had wanted him to go along. At least, Raphaela had. After all the talks he had given them about team spirit, about loyalty to fellow Force members, and about always being there when needed by a partner, he had violated his own rules of conduct and stayed behind at the Force facility.

Why?

Because he was ticked off at General Gallagher? Because Gallagher knew the importance of the training program and had thrown a monkey wrench in the works? Although, technically speaking, he should be upset at Governor Melnick since the three-day pass had been the chief executive's brainstorm.

Or could there be another, underlying reason?

Could it be he didn't want to become *too* attached to any of the new team?

He'd socialized as much as possible with the first Force squad, had tried to be a friend to each of them as well as their leader, and had grown to care a lot for most of them. And look at what happened! Five of them had died.

So was that the real reason he hadn't gone along to L.A.?"

Subconsciously, was he afraid of cementing emotional bonds that might be prematurely severed by the death of one of the team? Did he fear losing another member so much that he was unwilling to commit himself? Had he grown soft?

He'd learned one important lesson from the wise Family leader, Plato, and from his years of experience as the head of the Warriors. A lesson he'd apparently forgotten. Leadership entailed certain responsibilities, and foremost was the supreme responsibility to the ones being led. Dedication was paramount. A loner invariably made a poor leader because a loner couldn't relate well to other people. And relating, opening up and giving of oneself to others, in this case to those who relied upon his judgment to preserve their lives, was essential.

So get off your butt and relate, dummy!

The thought made Blade smile. He grabbed the phone and

dialed the three-digit number for the guard shack at the south gate.

"Sergeant Sirak here."

"Sergeant, this is Blade."

"Yes, sir?"

"I want a jeep to pick me up in five minutes."

"Right away, sir. And may I ask where the jeep will be taking you?"

"Into L.A. I'm going to take the governor up on his offer of three days of rest and relaxation."

"I don't blame you. Party hearty, sir."

CHAPTER EIGHT

None of them, not even Captain Havoc, had ever seen anything like the China White. Jaguarundi had never been to a nightclub in his life. Doc Madsen had frequented frontier bars and saloons where he plied his gambling trade. Sparrow Hawk was accustomed to the sedate life-style of rural Montana. Lobo, for all his bragging, had never set foot in a place remotely similar. And Raphaela, raised in the cloistered confines of the Mound, where the ruler of the Moles, the arrogant Wolfe, dictated the austere parameters of their existence, was positively bewildered.

A perpetual motion machine of swirling activity, the China White throbbed with a frenetic pulsebeat in rhythm to the pounding music of the heavy metal band. Flickering strobe lights lent the dance floor and the surrounding tables and booths the aspect of another dimension. Customers were dancing and laughing and chatting, creating a clamorous undercurrent of voices as a backdrop to the driving sounds of the Dead Mastodons.

The Force members halted next to a sign that read: PLEASE WAIT TO BE SEATED. They stared at the hectic scene before them, transfixed.

"That *is* music, isn't it?" Sparrow asked. "Now I'm not so sure."

"They don't even have poker tables here," Doc said. "How can they call this a classy club?"

"Do the lights have a short?" Jag inquired.

An attractive brunette, wearing a skimpy red outfit that barely covered her waist and caused her breasts to bulge, walked toward them smiling at the men in a seductive fashion. "Hello. I'm Susie, your hostess. A party of six?"

Lobo gawked at her huge bosom and rolled his eyes. "Oh, Momma! Hurt me!"

"A party of six," Havoc confirmed.

"Follow me," Susie said, and moved to the right.

Ogling her backside as she swayed off, Lobo clutched at his chest and groaned. "I think I'm in love."

"Down, boy, down," Jag joked.

"Behave yourself, brother," Sparrow said. "Remember Raphaela is with us."

"Oh, let him act like a fool if he wants," the Molewoman stated. "We all know how playful he can be."

"Playful?" Doc said, and snorted. "Harebrained is more like it."

They trailed after the hostess as she weaved among the tables along the south side of the room.

Susie glanced over her left shoulder. "Would you prefer a table or a booth?"

"A table near those dancers," Lobo said. "I like to see the women do their moves."

"A booth," Jag said, thinking he would prefer a quiet corner in the dim recesses.

"Which will it be?" Susie queried.

"A booth," Havoc said.

Lobo sighed, his gaze glued to a big-busted woman on the dance floor who seemed about to burst the seams of her skintight dress. "Dorks!" he mumbled. "I'm surrounded by dorks."

"What was that?" Raphaela asked.

"Nothin'."

The hostess escorted them to a booth in the far corner. "Your waitress will be with you in a bit," she stated, and left them.

"What a fox," Lobo breathed.

They squeezed into the booth, three to a side, with Havoc, Raphaela, and Lobo on the left. Jaguarundi took the inner seat on the right, as far from the lights as he could get. Then Sparrow Hawk and Doc Madsen sat down.

"Ain't this bitchin'?" Lobo commented.

Sparrow leaned over the table to be heard. "This is most confusing. How can these people hear themselves think with all this noise?"

"Who wants to think?" Lobo rejoined. "Thinkin' is for jerks. This is a place for people who want to live a little, who know how to get down and be funky."

"Be *what*?" Doc queried.

"Funky, bro. Funky. I wouldn't expect a corn-pone dude like you to know what it means."

"Listen to the English expert," Doc cracked.

"So now what do we do?" Raphaela asked, glancing from one to the other.

"We could order some drinks," Havoc suggested idly while surveying the club. He noticed there were an inordinate number of lovely women in short dresses who were circulating among the male patrons. Off to the left he spotted a man slipping a small packet of white powder into the palm of another man. "But I don't think we should stay very long."

"Are you kiddin'?" Lobo remarked. "I'm fixin' to spend the rest of my life here. This is heaven on earth."

"For some," Havoc said, and gazed at the far side of the club where a table larger than all the rest was located to the left of the stage. This table stood out because no other tables or booths were within fifteen feet of it, and because four men in dark suits were standing near one of the chairs, their eyes constantly roving over the crowd. In that chair sat a good-looking black man attired in an immaculate white suit. On his left sat a redheaded woman in a yellow gown. And at another chair was an immense black who had somehow lost his left hand. Instead of fingers, he had a wicked-looking metal pincer at the end of his arm. He wore a gray suit. He was also bald.

"I don't mind staying as long as no one notices me," Jag mentioned.

A shapely blonde whose only garment consisted of tassels on the tips of her breasts and a lacy napkin between her legs strolled over to their booth. "Hi. I'm Arlene. Can I get you anything?"

Lobo took one look at her, then covered his face with his hands and started to whine.

"What's wrong with your friend?" Arlene inquired.

"Him? We don't know him," Doc said.

"Yeah. He just wanted to sit with us because no one else would have him," Jag added.

"Comedians, huh? Well, what would you like to drink?"

"I would like a milk, please," Sparrow informed her.

"A milk sounds nice," Raphaela agreed.

Arlene looked from one to the other. "It sounds to me like you clowns have already had too much to drink. Now what would you really like?"

"Milk," Sparrow reiterated.

"We don't serve milk."

"What about herbal tea?"

Flustered, Arlene placed her left hand on her hip and jabbed her right index finger at the Flathead. "Look, Tonto. No milk, no tea. We serve hard liquor. That's it. You can have whiskey, scotch, vodka, rum, you name it. Or maybe you'd prefer a martini or a boilermaker—"

"I'll take a boilermaker," Havoc declared, then glanced at Lobo, who was eyeing the waitress while chewing on the sleeve of his black leather jacket. "Make that a double."

"I'll have a whiskey," Doc said.

"Do you have any prune juice?" Sparrow inquired.

Arelene hissed. "No juice, mister."

"I don't know what to have," Raphaela interjected, and stared at the captain. "Are boilermakers tasty?"

"I'd recommend you try a martini. One sip of a boilermaker and you won't be feeling any pain for a month."

Sparrow Hawk's interest perked up. "Ahhh. Boilermakers must contain medicinal properties."

"You don't do much drinking, do you, Tonto?" Arlene inquired.

"Very rarely," Sparrow said. "Too much alcohol clouds the mind."

"Then what happened to you? Did a buffalo fall on your head when you were a baby?" Arlene responded, and snickered at her own witticism.

"I'll take a martini," Raphaela announced.

"Okay," Arlene acknowledged, and stared at the left corner. "And what about you there, whiskers?"

"A beer would be nice."

"What brand?"

"Surprise me."

"Fair enough," Arlene replied, then focused on the Flathead. "Have you made up your mind yet?"

"Perhaps you could suggest a suitable drink?"

"I have just the thing," Arlene assured him. "You'll love it. Goes down smooth but has the kick of a mule. It's called a flaming sucker."

"I'll try one."

"Hallelujah!" Arlene said, and went to leave.

"Hey, what about me?" Lobo cried, finally finding his voice.

"What about you?"

"Why don't you bring me a real *man's* drink?"

"You're the masculine type, huh?"

"Invite me to your place sometime and I'll show you how manly I can be," Lobo proposed, leering lechereously.

"Not unless you provide proof of your rabies vaccination," Arlene retorted. "And I'll bring you a gin gimlet. That should be about your speed." She smiled, winked, and sashayed away.

"Did you hear that?" Lobo asked excitedly. "She likes me. She's warm for my form."

"She thinks your a putz," Jag commented.

"Bull-pukey, dude. She was makin' eyes at me," Lobo insisted. He shifted so he could see Havoc. "Hey, Cap. You know this city better than the rest of us."

"Yeah, so?"

"So where can I go to get my rabies vaccination?"

To everyone's surprise, the normally staid officer put his face in his hands and started to whine.

The Claw raised his metal appendage and scratched an itch on his cleft chin. "I can't believe she'd pull a stupid stunt like that."

"I can," Mr. Bad responded angrily, his handsome features contorted in suppressed rage. "Fayanne is a bimbo. I told you that. And she's a dead bimbo once I get my hands on her."

"The boys will find her."

"To think I trusted her once!" Mr. Bad spat, and pounded his right fist on the table. "I bought her the finest clothes money can buy. She lived in the lap of luxury. And this is how she repays me?"

"She's probably getting even with you for dumping her," Gloria Mundy mentioned.

Mr. Bad glanced at his latest squeeze, his lips tightening, his eyes flinty sparks. "Figured that out all by yourself, did you, slut?"

"There's no need to talk to me like that."

Mr. Bad reached over and clamped his left hand on her right wrist, then squeezed. "I'll talk to you any damn way I want, bitch."

"You're hurting me," the woman protested, striving to jerk her arm loose.

Sneering, Mr. Bad applied more pressure, digging his blunt nails into her skin, enjoying her pained visage. "You don't seem to be aware of the facts of life, Gloria, baby. Maybe a refresher course is in order," he said, and leaned toward her. "I didn't work my way up from the streets to become one of the most powerful men in L.A. only to have a snotty whore tell me what I can and can't do. If you weren't as dumb as a brick, you'd learn a lesson from Fayanne's behavior. You'd appreciate the severity of the consequences when you cross me."

"I wouldn't cross you. Honest," Gloria promised, grimacing and feebly twisting her arm. "Please let go of me."

Mr. Bad abruptly released her wrist. "Don't ever mouth off to me again or I'll throw your sorry ass back in the gutter where you belong. And from now on, you don't set foot in my condo unless by special invite. When I'm in the mood, I'll come across the hall and visit you. Got it?"

"I got it," Gloria snapped.

Sighing, Mr. Bad leaned back in his chair and glanced at the Claw. "A man can't get any respect anymore."

Gloria stood, rubbing her sore wrist, tears moistening her green eyes.

"Where do you think you're going?"

"To the ladies' room, if you don't mind!"

"Go. Good riddance," Mr. Bad said, and waved her away with his right hand. "I hope you drown in the toilet."

Gloria stared at the head of the Brothers for a moment, her lower lip quivering, then spun and stormed off toward the rest rooms situated at the northeast end of the club.

"You were kind of rough on her, weren't you?" the Claw mentioned idly.

"What if I was? She deserved it."

"Did she? Or were you taking out your feelings about Fayanne on Gloria?"

Mr. Bad looked at his bodyguard. "What the hell are you now, a friggin' psychiatrist?"

The Claw ignored the question. Instead, he inspected the razor-sharp inner edges of his custom-designed metal pincer, patterned after the pincers on a lobster, that had been affixed to his arm nine years ago after he had lost his hand in a rumble. The pincer had cost him a bundle, and he'd had to hustle to sell a lot of coke to pay for it, but the money had been well spent. Now he had the heaviest rep in the city. Now everyone knew about the Claw.

A soft sigh issued from Mr. Bad's lips. "I'm sorry, Claw. I had no reason to talk to you like that. You're right. I'm so damn mad about this Fayanne business that I'm not thinking straight."

"It'll all work out, Boss."

"I wish I had your confidence. Now that bastard Owsley knows the identity of every Brother. He can track them down at his leisure. Some of the boys might get a little nervous."

The Claw opened and closed his pincer with a loud snap. "I can take Dexter and Sheba and finish off Owsley for good."

"Too risky. That mansion of his is too well guarded."

"You thought the condo was well guarded, remember?"

"How was I to know that bitch would unlock the fire escape door? All my boys are posted in the lobby. No one can get through them. Except for Fayanne. She talked Webster into letting her go upstairs, when he knew damn well she wasn't supposed to be allowed past the ground floor," Mr. Bad said, and scowled. "I'll take care of Webster when this business is concluded."

"Web figured no harm would be done. He was tired of her pestering him, and he knew you weren't in. He thought she'd get it out of her system and leave him alone."

"Instead she must have unlocked the fire escape and snuck back later. But where did she get a key to my place? The damn bitch!"

"You need to take your mind off her," the Claw commented. "I've got something that'll cheer you up."

"What?"

"Have you scoped out the fox in the southwest corner?"

Mr. Bad turned in his chair and focused on the redhead in the far booth. "Not bad. She's better looking than Gloria. Who is she?"

"I've never seen her in here before."

"Who are those clowns with her? And why's that blond honky crying?"

"Beats me. I've never seen them either."

Mr. Bad adjusted his tie and smoothed his jacket. "Go get her. I'd like to meet her."

"What if she doesn't want to come?"

"Be serious."

The Claw stood, his six-foot-six frame uncoiling slowly, and headed for the booth.

CHAPTER NINE

"Hey, check out this dude with the can opener for a hand," Lobo cracked.

Captain Havoc had already noted the big black's steady advance in their direction. He suddenly wished he wasn't seated on the inside of the booth. The guy with the pincer appeared to be staring at Raphaela. "Heads up, people," he announced. "This could be trouble."

They all reacted differently. Jaguarundi pulled the brim of his hat lower, concealing his eyes. Doc Madsen placed his right hand in his lap and twisted sideways. Sparrow Hawk dropped his left arm near his left moccasin. And Lobo stuck his right hand partway up the left sleeve of his leather jacket.

Raphaela simply stared at the bald man, who was now less than 15 feet away. "What kind of trouble? What does he want?"

"We'll know in a sec," Lobo remarked, his expression suddenly uncharacteristically hard.

"I wish General Gallagher had let us bring weapons," Havoc mentioned.

None of the others said a word, although a slight grin flitted across Lobo's face.

"Good evening," the big black announced as he reached their booth. "Are you enjoying yourselves?"

"Yes," Raphaela responded.

"We're waitin' for our drinks," Lobo added coldly.

"Can we help you?" Havoc inquired.

"The owner would like to have a word with the lady," the man addressed Raphaela.

The Molewoman blinked. "Me?"

"Yes. If you would be so kind."

"Hold the phone, turkey," Lobo said. "Who's this owner?"

"She's not going anywhere," Havoc chimed in.

The big man regarded them for several seconds, his expression inscrutable. "Are you related to the lady?"

"We're her friends," Havoc replied. "We look out for her best interest. *All* of us." He indicated the others with a sweep of his arm.

"I see," the big black said, digesting the news, glancing from one to the other. "Well, I can assure you the lady is in no danger." He smiled and pointed at the table off by itself. "The owner is right there. You can keep an eye on her the whole time."

"Eye, hell," Lobo said. "Where Raphaela goes, we go."

"Is that your name?" the man asked the Molewoman, and when she nodded in response he grinned and said, "What a lovely name. It fits such a beautiful woman."

Raphaela blushed. "Oh, I'm not beautiful," she blurted out, embarrassed by the compliment.

Captain Havoc felt an almost irresistible impulse to smash the man with the pincer in the face. He intuitively distrusted the black. Every instinct told him that the man's suave behavior was a sham, that he was as deadly as a cobra. "If the owner wants to see Raphaela, tell him to come over here."

"Can't Raphaela talk for herself?"

"Of course I can," the Molewoman said defensively. "I don't need a baby-sitter."

The big man gave a slight bow. "Then why don't you come over to the owner's table. You have my personal guarantee that you won't be harmed."

Raphaela bit her lower lip and stared at the man in the white suit, then gazed at her friends, her uncertainty transparent. "I don't want to offend anyone," she said softly.

"If you want to go, go," Havoc stated. "But take one of us with you."

"You heard the lady," the man with the pincer stated. "She doesn't need a baby-sitter."

Doc Madsen, who had not uttered one word since the conversation started, suddenly spoke, his words uttered with a steely inflection, every word clipped and precise, his hazel eyes narrowed. "No one asked you."

The black stiffened and raised his pincer to chest height. He studied the gambler closely. "You think you can do it, mister?"

"Try me."

Everyone understood the implied meaning. Each one tensed, expecting violence to erupt, and for the span of ten seconds it appeared as if the big black was about to swipe his pincer at Madsen. But then another member of the Force enunciated five words that gave the man pause.

"Can you take us all?" Jaguarundi asked.

The big man hesitated, calculating the odds, noting the chilling gaze on each of the five. They were different from most, he decided. They weren't cowed by his mere presence. If he took out the cowboy, the others would be on him before he could blink. He wasn't afraid. He knew he could take them. But if they gave him as much trouble as he believed they could, some of the other customers might be inadvertently injured or the cops might be called. And Mr. Bad was a stickler for no hassles at the club. Reluctantly, he lowered his pincer and looked at the redhead. "Will you accept the owner's invitation or not?"

"I guess," Raphaela said, hoping to avoid the possibility of bloodshed by getting the man away from the booth. She nudged Lobo. "Excuse me."

The Clansman slipped out and stood. "I'm going with you," he announced.

"I'll be okay," Raphaela stated, smoothing her gown as she straightened.

"Take him," Captain Havoc directed with an air of finality.

"Follow me," the big black said, and grinned. "You can bring your pit bull." He walked off.

"What's a pit bull?" Lobo asked testily.

"Never mind," Havoc said. "Stick with her. And Raphaela, you stay within our sight at all times. Clear?"

"I'm perfectly capable of taking care of myself," Raphaela said.

"Do it."

"Who do you think you are? Blade?"

"If Blade was here, he'd tell you the same thing," Havoc declared. The thought gave him pause. Here he was, indirectly praising the Warrior, implicitly acknowledging yet again that Blade was a competent leader who truly cared about his people. How could he even contemplate betraying the giant?

"Take Lobo along," Jag urged. "Either that or we all go with you."

Raphaela faced them and tried to adopt a stern countenance, but the happiness she felt at their concern, their caring, weakened her resolve. So she simply shook her head in silent reproof, her eyes sparkling with affection the whole while, then trailed after the big black.

"Watch out for her, Lobo," Havoc instructed.

"You've got it, man. I don't trust that big dude worth spit." The Clansman hurried after Raphaela.

"I don't like this," Jag commented.

"Neither do I," Sparrow concurred.

"Maybe we all should mosey on over there," Doc suggested.

"No," Havoc said. "Raphaela is a grown woman. We can protect her, but we can't treat her like a child. We'll sit tight and hope nothing happens."

* * *

Raphaela nervously approached the table where the owner was seated. The man with the metal pincer had already reached it and was saying something in the owner's ear. She wondered if she should have accepted the invitation, if she had made a mistake. Havoc obviously hadn't wanted her to go, and he was a better judge of others, of their true natures and motivations. She would be the first to admit her inexperience in affairs of the world. But how was she to learn to relate to others without the experience of meeting new people? She gazed at the two men and suppressed her anxiety.

"I'm right behind you," Lobo declared.

"Thanks for coming."

"You're not mad?"

"Why should I be mad? I kind of like having five goofy brothers to watch over me. I never had any real family at the Mound."

"Hey, what are friends for?" Lobo responded.

They took several more strides.

"And who are you callin' goofy?"

Raphaela mustered a smile and halted two yards from the man in the white suit. "Hello. You wanted to see me?"

"Most definitely," the owner replied, rising and motioning at the chair next to his. "Have a seat. Claw told me your name is Raphaela. I'm Mr. Bad."

"Mr. Bad?" Raphaela repeated quizzically, and heard Lobo burst into laughter.

"Are you jivin' us? What kind of idiot names himself Mr. Bad?" the Clansman queried. "And this other dork is named Claw? Prune-face would be better."

Raphaela saw both men visibly check a surge of anger. Mr. Bad glared at Lobo for an uncomfortably long time.

"Do you have any idea who I am?" the owner snapped.

"Yeah. This joint is yours. Righteous place you've got here."

"I'm a very powerful man in this city. You don't want to antagonize me."

"Should I tremble now or later?"

Mr. Bad frowned. "You're making a mistake. I won't

tolerate disrespect from anyone, least of all a nothing like you."

Raphaela took a step forward. "If you're going to insult my friend, I'm leaving. I'm tired of all this squabbling."

"My apologies. But you can see he provoked me," Mr. Bad replied. "Please. Have a seat. Both of you."

Raphaela sat down, and Lobo did likewise to her left. She observed that the one called Claw stayed standing although the owner took his seat again. She also noticed the four other men hovering nearby. Who were they? What had she gotten herself into now?

"You must be curious about why I invited you over," Mr. Bad mentioned, taking his seat once more.

"Yes," Raphaela admitted.

"It's because I'm a man who genuinely appreciates beauty, and you're a ravishing woman."

"Thank you," Raphaela said, confused by the flattery. She wasn't accustomed to having men compliment her so freely, and she blamed all this unusual attention on her new gown. She should never have let that saleswoman convince her to buy such a revealing evening dress.

"I'm sincere," Mr. Bad stressed, smiling warmly. He indicated the dance floor with a bob of his head. "I see lovely women in here every night of the week. Few are as stunning as you are."

Lobo yawned. Loudly.

"I would love to be able to talk to you in private," Mr. Bad proposed. "I have a condo near here. Perhaps you would be interested in going there?"

"A condo?" Raphaela said, puzzled by the reference. What the heck was a condo?

"I can have caviar and champagne brought up," Mr. Bad said. "This club is hardly the proper atmosphere in which to get to know one another."

And abruptly comprehension dawned. Raphaela felt her pulse quicken. The owner was making a pass at her! He was inviting her to his place for an intimate night together! The realization startled her. She had never viewed herself as exceptionally attractive, and with a singular exception she had never been sexually approached by any man. Of course, her aunt had had a lot to do with that. The witch had actively discouraged every suitor except one, and that one had been the source of her everlasting shame.

"Is something wrong?" Mr. Bad inquired. "Have I offended you?"

Raphaela shook her head, stunned to perceive she must have let her innermost feelings show. She had determined long ago never to tell another living soul about the horror she had undergone, not to let anyone know about her degradation. "I'm fine," she mumbled.

"Are you sure?" Lobo interjected.

Another man hastened over to the table, a skinny white man in a green suit. "Excuse me, Boss," he declared deferentially.

Mr. Bad looked up, peeved at the interruption. "Spike, this had better be important."

"I'm sorry to bother you, but Ms. Mundy has locked herself in the ladies' and she's threatening to slash her wrists with a razor."

"She's *what*?" Mr. Bad hissed, and came out of his chair with his fists clenched.

"We've tried to talk her out, Boss, but she just won't budge. There are a lot of women waiting to use the rest room. What do you want us to do?"

Mr. Bad glanced at Raphaela, maintaining his composure with a supreme effort. "Would you stay here until I return? I must deal with a trivial matter. It will only take a few minutes."

"I guess so."

"Thank you," Mr. Bad said, and stormed off to the northeast with the Claw, the man named Spike, and the four men in dark suits all in tow.

"Now what do you suppose that was all about?" Raphaela wondered aloud.

"Who cares?" Lobo responded. "I say we go back to our booth and let these jerks play with themselves."

"Why must you always be so crude?"

"Who's crude? I just call it like it is. You've got to remember, Raphy baby, that I spent almost my entire life in the toughest gang in the Twin Cities. I lived in the gutter, and I saw people for what they really are."

"Which is?"

"They're worse than animals, babe. When you get down to the nitty-gritty, most people are only lookin' out for number one. They'll screw you over every chance you get."

"That's not true. Am I trying to screw you?"

"I wish."

"What?"

"Nothin'. No, you're a decent chick."

"And what about Blade and the rest? Are they trying to screw you over?"

"No."

"They're your friends and so am I. Never forget that, Lobo."

"I'll try not to."

"I know being in the Force is rough on you. It's rough on all of us. We have to think of ourselves as one big, happy family. How else are we going to survive a whole year together?"

"Beats the hell out of me," Lobo said, and glanced toward their booth. "Look, babe, let's go back. I don't like it here."

"But I promised Mr. Bad."

Lobo sighed and tapped his fingers on the tabletop. "Raphy, I know you were raised by the Moles, and I know they're not the brightest chumps who ever waltzed down the pike, but hasn't it occurred to you that this guy isn't the kind you want to be messin' with?"

"He seems nice enough," Raphaela said defensively.

"Oh, right. Then why does everyone call him *Mr. Bad*?"

"You took the name Lobo, and you're a real peach."

The Clansman snorted and gazed off at the rest rooms. The crowd prevented him from seeing Bad and company. "What's it going to take to wake you up, girl? Life is a bitch. Everyone ain't nice and sweet like you."

Raphaela gazed around at the dancers and the throng of

patrons. "You're worried over nothing. We're in a public place. What can happen?"

As if in answer, ten men suddenly streamed through a door located in the southeast corner of the club, each man armed with a machine gun, a shotgun, or an assault rifle, and before anyone quite grasped their intention and could dive for cover, the ten opened fire.

CHAPTER TEN

Captain Havoc glimpsed a commotion out of the corner of his right eye and turned in time to see the armed men enter the nightclub. Mere seconds before the firing erupted he dove out from the booth, sliding to the floor, and yelled to his companions, "Get down!"

The next instant pandemonium erupted as the men cut loose, shooting indiscriminately into the patrons, blasting men and women alike. The blasting of the guns mingled with the shrieks and screams of the dying and the wounded, creating a raucous din, a metallic symphony of death. As the ten men fired they advanced farther into the club, their bullets mowing a path through the throng. Those customers not hit were frantically striving to make themselves scarce, and the ten gunmen found it easy to race across the previously packed dance floor toward the large table all by itself to the left of the stage.

Toward Lobo and Raphaela.

"Down, babe! Down!" the Clansman cried, rising and

hauling her from her chair. He shoved her under the table, hoping to put her out of the line of fire, then spun toward the intruders, his right hand reaching under his left sleeve. He saw four people in front of him go down, their bodies perforated and spurting blood, and his fingers were just closing on his concealed NATO when something slammed into his forehead with the force of a sledgehammer and he was hurled backwards onto the table, his senses swimming. He heard Raphaela shout his name, and his last thought before the world faded into darkness was that he hoped his friends had seen him go down and would come to her aid.

But they hadn't.

Captain Havoc looked to his left, where Sparrow, Doc, and Jag were lying prone, then at the swirling mass of confusion and bloodshed before him. His logical military mind formulated a dozen questions: Who were these men? What did they want? Why were they murdering innocent bystanders? What had the Force gotten itself into?

The majority of the patrons were fleeing in stark panic toward the corridor to the outside, some helping those who had been wounded, but most pushing and shoving one another in their frenzied eagerness to escape the spreading carnage.

Havoc took a risk. The wild crowd temporarily screened him from the gunmen, so he quickly rose and scanned the club, searching for Lobo and Raphaela. The sight he saw chilled him to the marrow. The Clansman was lying on top of the table, blood on his head, and three of the gunmen had the Molewoman in their grasp and were hauling her back in the direction they had came. Seeing her in danger shattered his customary prudence, and he started forward, bellowing, "They're taking Raphaela!" Heedless of his safety he waded into the throng, trying to break through them to the dance floor to intercept the trio ushering her out.

As yet, no one had fired a shot at the attackers.

The living wall of desperate patrons prevented Havoc from getting in the clear. Supremely frustrated, watching the three gunmen cover yards while he covered inches, he lost control and began to strike and batter the customers aside, using the karate skills he had honed to a consummate degree, never going for a death blow, only using sufficient strength to stun those who wouldn't move out of his way. He covered several yards before he realized he wasn't alone.

Doc Madsen, Sparrow Hawk, and Jaguarundi were driving a wedge into the mob, working together, standing side by side and hurling all comers from their path.

Havoc angled to assist them. He could see Raphaela and the three gunmen were already halfway across the dance floor, being covered by the seven other killers. They had ceased shooting, apparently feeling they had achieved their goal, and were slowly retreating.

Damn them!

Dozens and dozens of bodies littered the dance floor and the spaces between the tables. Even several of the band members had been slain. The drummer had pitched forward into his drums, and a guitarist had collapsed onto an amp that was spitting red and orange sparks.

Havoc realized it would take a miracle for the four of them to reach Raphaela before the gunmen made good their escape. He pushed a portly man out of the way, then barreled past two terrified women, and suddenly a narrow cleared space materialized between him and the dance floor. There stood one of the killers, an M-16 clutched in his hands.

The gunman saw the officer at the same moment and elevated the barrel to fire.

For a sinking second Havoc expected to feel slugs ripping through his torso, and he heard a gun boom but it wasn't the M-16. Instead, the shot came from his left and the killer took a bullet high in the head and stumbled several feet, then fell, the M-16 clattering on the floor. Havoc looked to the left.

Doc Madsen had his Smith and Wesson Model 586 Distinguished Combat Magnum in his right hand. His shot had caused everyone in front of him to scatter, and he darted into the open. The trio who had captured Raphaela were almost to the door through which they had entered, and the remaining killers were backing in the same direction. Madsen never bothered to calculate the odds. He crouched and fired, three shots cracking almost as one, and three of the gunmen went down. He immediately flattened and rolled to his left, anticipating the killers would come after him.

They did.

Three more sprinted toward the Cavalryman, intent on taking revenge for their dead associates. They closed rapidly, holding their fire to ensure they wouldn't miss the still-rolling figure, and they were still advancing when a furry form hurtled out of nowhere to land among them.

Jaguarundi had lost his hat in the initial scuffle to break through the crowd. Uncomfortable in any type of clothing, his movements impaired by the restricting suit, he had halted just long enough to rip his new garments from his body, shredding the fabric with his nails, and then seen Doc slay the first killer. His steely sinews propelled him toward the gunmen in a series of vaulting leaps, and he was almost over the last of the crowd when Doc shot the three other butchers. Now he alighted among the onrushing hit men and went to work, slashing right and left, ripping his nails into the throats of two of them before the startled men could react to the shock of confronting a hybrid.

The last of the gunmen swung toward Jag and pointed a shotgun. "Die, freak!" he roared, and a millisecond later stiffened and staggered a stride, then dropped onto his knees, his eyes wide, his mouth opening and closing.

For a moment Jag didn't understand, and then he saw Sparrow appear behind the assassin and wrench a hunting knife from the man's back. The Flathead then knocked the man onto the floor. "Thanks," Jag called, and swung toward the doorway in the southeast corner.

Raphaela and the three killers were just disappearing into a hallway beyond.

Jag took off in pursuit, and as the fleetest Force member he reached the doorway before his friends. The door hung slightly ajar, and he grabbed the knob and pulled. Only his superb feline instincts saved his life, because as he opened the door a small voice in the back of his mind warned him to move and he did, ducking to the left.

A volley of automatic fire whizzed through the doorway.

Jag glanced at his teammates, but they were all right, each one flat on the floor, evidently having thrown themselves there when he took hold of the door handle. Blade's training was paying off, he thought, then peeked into the hallway.

At the far end a door was closing.

Raphaela! Her name rang shrilly in his mind as he bounded down the hall, passing a utility closet and a supply room. He came to the door and discovered that the lock and handle had been smashed when the ten killers made their entry into the club. This door, like the last, was open about an inch. He hesitated before throwing it wide, expecting to receive the same treatment as he had previously, and in the few seconds he paused he heard the distinct roar of an engine throbbing to life.

They were making their getaway!

Alarmed, he hauled on the door and sprang into the cool night, finding himself on some sort of receiving platform. There were two dead men nearby, both shot through the back. Past the platform lay a parking lot, and racing from the lot was a big limousine.

No!

Jag dashed to the edge of the platform, realizing there was no way he could catch the speeding vehicle. He watched helplessly as the limo took a left on screeching tires and sped off.

"Damn! Was that them?" a familiar voice queried anxiously to the hybrid's rear.

Frowning, Jag pivoted and nodded at Havoc. Doc and Sparrow were coming through the doorway. "What do we do now?"

"First, we check on Lobo," Havoc replied, and headed inside again.

"Why don't we steal one of these other cars and follow the limousine?" Jag asked, following.

"By the time I could hot-wire one of those cars, the limo will be long gone," Havoc said. He glanced at the Cavalryman and the Flathead as he passed them. "I thought the general told us not to bring weapons."

"I never go anywhere without my six-gun," Doc stated. "And I reckon I don't much care what old mealy-mouth says one way or the other."

Sparrow grinned and hefted his knife. "Do you mean this? Among my tribe a knife is considered a tool, and the general did *not* say we couldn't bring our tools."

Havoc smiled, then increased his speed, jogging all the way to the dance floor. Most of the patrons were gone, except for a few stragglers, the moaning and groaning wounded, and the dead. He dashed to the large table, hearing the others pounding on his heels, and drew up in consternation when he saw the blood trickling from a gash in the Clansman's right temple. "No!" he exclaimed, and grabbed Lobo's right wrist to feel for a pulse.

"Is he still alive?" Jag inquired.

Havoc motioned for silence while pressing his fingertips to the Clansman's skin. Lobo was so still, his chest not even moving. But at the same second Havoc found a weak pulse, the loquacious malcontent gasped, inhaling deep into his lungs, and his eyelids fluttered. "Lobo!" Havoc exclaimed. "Can you hear me?"

"What happened?" the Clansman responded, the words barely audible. "Did Blade get tired of all my goofin' off?"

"No. Don't you remember? You were shot. Raphaela has been taken."

Lobo's eyes snapped open. "Those bastards took her? Why?"

"We don't know yet," Havoc said. He inspected the gash and was relieved to discover it was a flesh wound, nothing more. The blood flow had already started to taper off. "We've got to bandage you and go after Raphaela."

"Forget about me," Lobo said, and tried to rise. Dizziness swamped him and his head sagged.

"We'll lend you a hand," Doc offered, and took hold of the Clansman's left arm.

Havoc nodded, and they raised Lobo to a sitting posture.

"Sparrow, find something we can use to bandage his wound."

"On my way," the Flathead said, and departed.

"Jag, go see if you can find that bozo in the white suit or the guy with the claw. They might know what this is all about," Havoc said.

"And if they don't want to come, can I tear them into itty-bitty pieces?"

"No. We need them alive."

"Spoilsport," Jag muttered, and headed in the direction he'd seen the man in white go.

"I'll be fine," Lobo insisted. "I don't need no damn bandage. We've got to find Raphaela."

"First things first," Havoc replied. "We have to learn where those clowns are taking her, and hope they don't harm her before we get there."

"Anybody who hurts her is dog meat," Lobo vowed. He gingerly ran his fingers over the bullet crease, then stared at the blood on his hand. "I owe those suckers bad."

"We all do," Doc concurred.

"I should call Blade," Havoc mentioned, and gazed around for sign of a telephone. None were visible, and he was about to go in search of a booth when he spied Sparrow Hawk returning, a strip of white cloth in the Flathead's left hand.

"I cut this off a tablecloth," Sparrow informed them as he approached. He slowed and extended his arm. "It's the best I can do on the spur of the moment. At least it's clean."

Havoc took the cloth and proceeded to loop it around Lobo's head, binding the wound tightly, staunching the flow of blood. "Is that too tight?" he asked.

"No. Let's go find Raphaela."

"Be patient."

"We can't afford to be wastin' time, dude."

"Don't you think I know that?"

Doc Madsen suddenly straightened. "Hey. Look."

They stared toward the rest rooms. Jaguarundi was already on his way back, a skinny man wearing a green suit clasped in his iron grasp. The man was too petrified to even contemplate resisting.

"Who's this?" Havoc queried.

"His name's Spike," Jag answered. "I found him in the ladies' room, and I remembered seeing him talk to that bastard in the white suit shortly before the crap hit the fan."

"Yeah," Lobo chimed in. "He's one of Mr. Bad's men."

"Who?" Havoc asked.

"Mr. Bad. The chump in the white suit."

Havoc walked over to the hybrid and the prisoner, then seized the front of Spike's shirt and slammed him into the table, ramming the henchman's spine against the wood.

Spike cried out and clutched at his back.

"I need answers, friend," Havoc said, his voice low and gravelly. "If you don't provide them, you'll be one sorry son of a bitch."

In pain, his features livid, Spike glared at the blond man. "Go to hell."

A curious, cold grin creased the officer's mouth. "Do you see this?" Havoc remarked, and held his right hand up, his thick fingers rigid, the tips curled slightly inward.

"It's a hand. So what?" Spike said defiantly.

Havoc swept his right hand in a tight, controlled arc, driving his rock-hard fingers into the henchman's ribs, burying his hand to the knuckles.

An exquisite squeal of anguish burst from Spike's thin lips and he doubled over, wheezing and sputtering, spittle lining his mouth.

With a brutal wrench of his right hand, Havoc jerked the man erect. "You're not paying attention, asshole. Do you want me to do that again?"

"No!" Spike blubbered, shaking his head vigorously.

"Good. Then listen closely. I can break bricks and six-inch boards with my bare hands, and if you don't cooperate I'm going to do the same thing to each of your ribs. Got me?"

Spike nodded.

"What happened to Mr. Bad and that guy with the metal pincer?"

"They cut out when the shooting started, mister. They had just got Mr. Bad's old lady out of the john. Mr. Bad wanted to stay and fight, but Claw persuaded him to get the hell out of here. Claw thought the Barons might be attacking in force and he didn't want Mr. Bad to be hurt. Most of our soldiers are out on the street."

"The Barons? Do you mean this attack was gang-related?"

"Of course. Who else would be crazy enough to hit the Brothers at our own club?"

Havoc straightened. The whole incident now made sense. Except for one aspect. "Why did the Barons take our friend Raphaela?"

"How should I know?"

Suddenly Havoc remembered the other woman he had seen at Mr. Bad's table, the other *redheaded* woman, and he tensed. "What does Mr. Bad's old lady look like?"

Spike's brow knit at the unusual question. "Gloria? Oh, she's a stone fox, man. Great tits."

Havoc locked his left hand on the man's throat. "What color is her hair, moron?"

"Red!" Spike answered quickly, startled by the fire blazing from the blond man's eyes. "It's red! Honest!"

"Son of a bitch," Havoc declared bitterly, and released the Brother.

"Are you thinking what I think you're thinking?" Jag inquired.

Havoc nodded. "The Barons took Raphaela by mistake."

"And that mistake will cost them," Doc vowed.

The officer glanced at Spike. "Where would the Barons take her?"

"I don't know."

"Don't lie to me."

"I don't!" Spike whined. "They could take her anywhere."

"The Barons must have a headquarters, a base of operations," Havoc noted.

"There's Owsley's mansion."

"Who?"

"Owsley, man. The head of the Barons. He's got a mansion somewhere up in West Hollywood. I don't know exactly where."

"Who would know?"

"Well, Mr. Bad for sure, and probably Claw or Dex and Sheba, but they all took off for Mr. Bad's condo."

"And do you know where the condo is located?"

"Of course," Spike responded arrogantly. "You think I don't know where my own boss lives?" He saw the blond smile, a strangely unnerving expression, and perceived his mistake. "No! I can't!"

"You will," Havoc said.

"They'll kill me if I do."

"We'll kill you if you don't."

Spike glanced at each of them in turn, noting their hard expressions. Any one of them appeared quite capable of offing him without a second thought, but the hybrid really worried him. The thing smirked and raised its hands, then clicked its long fingernails together. Spike got the message and gulped. "All right, man. You win. I'll take you to the condo."

"Somehow I thought you would."

"But I want you to promise me something."

"What?"

"Keep that freak away from me. He gives me the creeps," Spike said anxiously.

"He'll leave you alone if you behave yourself," Havoc replied. "But if you try any tricks, anything at all, he'll gut you."

Jaguarundi beamed. "Gut, hell! I haven't tasted human gonads in ages."

Spike looked down toward his jewels, imagined those tapered teeth tearing into him, and shuddered. "You're kidding, right? You wouldn't really eat my balls, would you?"

A feral snarl issued from the hybrid and he leaned closer. "Try me."

CHAPTER ELEVEN

Seymour was engaged in checking the cubbyholes for a missing key to Room 1195 when a low voice addressed him from behind, surprising him because he hadn't heard anyone approach the registration desk. He almost jumped.

"Where can I find the Force?"

"Who wants to know?" Seymour responded, peering into one last slot.

"*I* do."

"And who might you—" Seymour began, rotating on his heels, his eyes becoming the size of walnuts when he saw the man standing in front of the counter, the biggest man he had ever laid eyes on, a movable mountain endowed with layer upon layer of bulging muscle, a giant with dark hair and gray eyes attired in a black leather vest and fatigue pants. There were two conspicious bulges under the vest, one above either hip. "My word!" he exclaimed.

"I'm looking for the Force," the giant reiterated, and held out his left hand. In the brawny palm rested an identification card.

Seymour took one look and almost stopped breathing. "Blade!"

"And who are you?"

"Seymour Verloc, at your service, sir. Your friends have been assigned the Presidential Suite and the Ambassador Suite on the top floor."

"Thank you," the giant said, and started to turn.

"But they're not there now," Seymour added hastily.

"Where are they?"

Seymour coughed and folded his hands on top of the counter. "They decided to go out and celebrate, and I suggested a club quite popular with our younger patrons. It's very . . . bitchin'."

The giant's eyebrows arched. "Bitchin'?"

"That's a term I picked up from Mr. Lobo," Seymour said. "He can be quite a colorful character."

"You don't know the half of it. What's the name of this club?"

"The China White."

"Where is it located?"

Seymour glanced at the entrance, through the glass doors at the waiting cabs parked outside. "I'll tell you what, sir. I'll do better than give you the address. I will personally escort you outside and get a taxi for you."

"That's very nice of you."

"Only the best for you, Mr. Blade. I know about some of your exploits, sir. I've read the accounts in the newspapers."

"They tend to exaggerate."

Seymour regarded the giant's physique for a moment. "If you ask me, sir, they don't do you justice." He hurried around the counter and motioned for the giant to follow. Every person in the lobby was staring at them, and Seymour held his head proudly, happy to be observed in such illustrious company.

The doorman had the door wide open way before they reached the entrance.

"Your friends weren't expecting you," Seymour mentioned as they reached the sidewalk. He saw three cabbies conversing near the foremost taxi and walked over to them. Two of them glanced at him, then gaped at the giant, but the third, a portly driver, was facing in the opposite direction. "Excuse me."

"What is it, bub?" the portly driver asked over his left shoulder. He was about to take a bite from a triple-decker mayo-and-corned-beef sandwich.

"Didn't one of you gentlemen take the Force to the China White?"

"You mean those weirdos? Yeah, I took them," the portly man said, the words muffled by the food crammed in his mouth. "What of it, Pops?"

"You need to take this man there right away."

"I don't *need* to do nothing," the driver snapped, and turned around. Only then did he spy the seven-foot figure standing behind the desk clerk, and he seemed to experience unexpected difficulty in talking. "H—h—him?"

"Right away," Seymour emphasized.

"Hey, whatever he wants, he gets," the driver declared. He stepped to his cab and opened the rear door. "Here you go, mister. I'll have you to that club in no time."

The giant nodded and slid into the vehicle.

In an amazing display of speed for one so out of shape, the driver darted around the taxi to his door and climbed in. He tossed the rest of his sandwich onto the front seat, twisted the ignition key, and in seconds they were on their way. "Say, aren't you the guy I've read about? The one they call Blade?" he inquired while gazing in the rear view mirror.

"That's me."

"Then those six I took to the club must be the rest of the Force!"

"Yep."

"I never would've believed it."

"Why not?"

"Well, for one thing, the newspapers never said nothing about no nympho."

CHAPTER TWELVE

"That's the place?"

"It is," Spike assured the blond guy. "Honest. I swear it. Mr. Bad's condo is on the fifteenth floor."

Havoc scrutinized the structure, debating their next move. They had ridden to within two hundred feet of the building in a battered old Ford belonging to the Brother, and now they were standing next to the parked vehicle, shrouded by the night, a cool breeze blowing from the northwest. "Does Mr. Bad own the entire high-rise?"

"Yeah."

"So there must be guards posted in the lobby?"

Spike nodded.

"How many?"

"It varies, man. Right now, with the war on and all, there must be a dozen or so."

The captain placed his hands on his hips. "You mentioned something about most of the gang members being out on the street?"

"That's right. They're out looking for Fayanne Raymond.

The bitch turned over and sold Mr. Bad's books to Owsley. Mr. Bad wants her real bad. He's offering ten grand to whoever brings her in."

"Then that's the reason there weren't enough Brothers at the club to repulse the attack," Havoc deduced. He spied a fire escape on the south side of the structure. "Are the fire escape doors kept locked?"

"Usually."

"What are we waiting for?" Doc Madsen asked impatiently. "Let's just barge in there and get the information we need."

"We can't afford a blunder at this stage of the game, not with Raphaela's life on the line," Havoc said. "Jag, I want you to keep an eye on our friend here while I check out the lobby."

"With pleasure," the hybrid said, and stepped closer to the Brother. "You will be a good little boy, won't you?"

"Anything you say," Spike responded.

"Do you want to take my gun?" Doc offered.

"No, thanks," Havoc answered, and walked toward the building.

"But you're not armed," Sparrow pointed out.

"I have my hands and my feet."

The vehicle traffic on the adjacent avenue was moderately heavy, and there were scores of pedestrians moving in both directions. Street lamps were spaced at 50-foot intervals, affording a fair degree of illumination.

Havoc strolled casually along, his hands in his front pockets, whistling the tune to the classic song "Secret Agent Man," one of his all-time favorites. He studied the layout, seeking any weakness he could take advantage of to gain entry without having to resort to more violence. Not that he disliked violence. Quite the contrary. He had made a career out of being one of the most lethal soldiers in the California military. But without adequate firepower, the Force would be going up against nearly insurmountable odds in assaulting Mr. Bad's stronghold.

The building had been set back approximately 20 yards from the avenue. A wide walk, lined with trees, led to the entrance. A narrow strip of lawn bordered the trees on both sides.

Maintaining his air of nonchalance, Havoc turned down the walk and ambled toward a pair of glass doors. Visible inside were a half-dozen men lounging about in chairs, on a couch, and standing next to a small counter.

One of the men spied the officer and alerted his comrades.

Havoc saw more men appear, and although there were no guns in evidence, he surmised they were all armed. He plastered an inane smile on his face and walked boldly to the doors, then opened the one on the right.

"What do you want?" a burly black dressed all in black leather demanded gruffly.

"I was hoping I could use your phone," Havoc said pleasantly. "I've got a flat tire and I'd like to call a garage."

"No phone," the black said.

Havoc glanced at the counter, where a telephone rested near the wall. "Then what's that?"

Several of the Brothers converged on the officer. The spokesman walked up and poked Havoc in the chest. "You don't hear so good, sucker. I told you we don't have a phone you can use."

"Oh," Havoc said, playing the role of a typical motorist to the hilt. He counted 11 men in the lobby. "Well, if you're going to be stuffy about it, I'll find a phone elsewhere."

"You do that."

Adopting an angry expression, Havoc spun and exited. He grinned as he walked to the avenue and took a left. The others were waiting expectantly for his return.

"What did you find out?" Sparrow inquired.

"There are eleven men on the ground floor, too many for us to take on without weapons," Havoc revealed.

Spike snickered. "Then why don't you let me go and we'll forget all about this?"

"Shut your mouth," Doc snapped, and looked at Havoc. "We need to find out where those varmin took Raphaela."

"Don't you think I know that?"

"Every delay puts her life more in danger."

"I know that too."

"Then I take it you won't have any objections if I call the shots for a few minutes?" Doc commented. He walked to the driver's door and stared at the steering column to verify the keys were still in the car.

"What do you think you're doing?" Havoc queried.

"Getting us inside," the Cavalryman replied, and got into the Ford.

"How do you propose to accomplish that feat?" Havoc asked.

"Watch and learn," Doc said out the open window. He stared at the dash. "Now let's see if I can recollect those driving lessons Blade gave me."

Perplexed, Havoc stepped off the curb. "What the hell are you doing?"

The engine abruptly kicked over. Doc gave a little wave, glanced back to ensure he could merge with the traffic flow without a problem, and pulled out.

"Where's that cowboy going with my wheels, man?" Spike questioned.

Jaguarundi cackled and sprinted toward the building. "Last one there misses out on all the fun."

Sparrow Hawk took off too.

"They'll need me," Lobo said, and managed several strides before he was forced to halt by a wave of vertigo. He swayed and almost fell.

"You stay with me," Havoc stated. He took hold of Spike's arm and almost tore the limb from its socket when he hauled the Brother after him, his gaze on Doc as the gambler drove toward the stronghold, uncertain of what the Cavalryman had in mind.

Jag and Sparrow were cutting across the lawn to the front doors.

The front doors! Havoc suddenly understood and started to run, but their prisoner dug in his heels, slowing him down.

"What the hell are you assholes doing?" Spike queried angrily. "You'd better not put a dent in my wheels."

"How about if we put a dent in you?" Havoc responded, and whipped his right arm upward, delivering a *Uraken* blow to the Brother's jaw, the back of his knuckles cracking

Spike's teeth together and rocking the man's head backward. He drove his right elbow into Spike's ribs, doubling the Brother over, then rammed his right knee into Spike's face. The skinny man dropped, senseless. Instantly Havoc took off for the condo, but the delay had cost him. He was already too far away to do more than witness Madsen's gambit.

The Ford abruptly accelerated and performed a sharp turn, bumping over the curb and roaring down the wide walk as Doc floored the gas pedal. He pressed on the raucous horn and held it in.

Hearing the strident noise, the 11 men inside the lobby came to the front doors and peered out, many fingering the weapons they carried concealed under their jackets. Several of them recognized the car as Spike's, and one of them even voiced a complaint: "What the hell is that idiot doing now?" For a few precious seconds they failed to realize they were being attacked, not until one of their number cried, "Hey! That's not Spike!" Then they all broke and tried to scatter out of the path of the onrushing metallic battering ram. By then it was too late.

Doc had the car doing 58 miles an hour when it crashed into the glass doors, shattering the panes and buckling the frame in a tremendous collison, and still the vehicle kept going. The fender and the grill slammed into the packed Brothers and sent them flying, while several were ground underneath the front end, screaming as the tires crunched over them. Not until the Ford hit the wall across from the entrance did the vehicle finally stop.

Seven of the guards were out of commission, either dead or too injured to fight. The remaining four pulled their weapons and tried to fire.

The driver's door shot wide and a black form dove to the floor, a pearl-handled revolver in his right hand, and even as he executed the dive he squeezed off two shots.

A pair of Brothers went down.

A tall man armed with an Uzi trained the weapon on their attacker and was about to cut loose when something pounced on his back and drove him to his knees. Enraged, he twisted, and his fury changed to fear when he saw the bestial visage above him.

"Surprise!" Jag said, and slashed his nails twice, ripping the man's throat apart. Blood gushed forth, spattering his fur coat.

The sole guard still erect swung toward the hybrid, a SIG/SAUER P230 clenched in his right hand. A gleaming object streaked from the left and thudded into his chest, and he looked down to find a large knife imbedded to the hilt. Bewilderment flitted across his features and he pitched onto his face as his chest seemed to implode. He screamed and turned onto his side, blood spurting from his mouth, and died.

"Thanks, Geronimo," Jag quipped.

"The name is Sparrow Hawk," the Flathead reminded him, and swiftly retrieved his knife, yanking the weapon out and wiping the blade clean on his victim's clothes.

Jag snickered and advanced to the counter. "We got them all," he said, scanning the lobby, admiring their handiwork. Several of the Brothers were groaning in pain.

"Should we put them out of their misery?" Sparrow inquired.

"Forget them," Doc said rising. He began to reload the spent rounds using the cartridges he had stuffed in his pockets before departing the Force compound.

Just then the telephone started ringing.

"Want me to answer it?" Jag said.

"No," Doc replied. "It might be someone upstairs wondering what all the ruckus was about. We've got to get to the top floor."

"Where's Twinkletoes?" Jag wondered, and gazed at the entrance as Havoc and Lobo arrived. "There you are! Where have you been? Taking a leak?"

The captain entered the lobby, disregarding the barbs. He stared at the ruined car, then at the bodies, and finally at the Cavalryman. "You could have been killed."

"And what do you think will happen to Raphaela if we don't get our butts in gear?"

"Let's go," Havoc said, and made for the elevator.

The telephone was still ringing when they commenced their ascent.

"There's no answer, boss," Dexter reported, and hung up the phone.

"We've got to get out of here," the Claw declared.

"I'm through running," Mr. Bad responded harshly. "If the Barons are on their way up, let's give them a reception they'll never forget."

"We can't stay," the Claw stated. "If the Barons have snuffed Web and the other guards, then they must be attacking with every soldier they've got. We wouldn't stand a chance."

Mr. Bad glanced at his bodyguard. "I know you're not yellow, so why do you want to run?"

"If you get racked, what's left for the rest of us? The Brothers are nothing without you. Yeah, we can stay and take them on, but if they outnumber us, then they'll nail us in the end. Why not stay alive and get our revenge on Owsley?"

Hatred contorted Mr. Bad's countenance. "You've got a point. I want that son of a bitch to suffer before he dies. I want to look in his eyes and laugh in his fat face as I stick it to him."

"Then come on," the Claw urged. "We don't have that much time."

"Hey! What about me?" Gloria Mundy called out from her seat on the sofa.

"Jump off the damn roof for all I care," Mr. Bad snapped. He looked at his two lieutenants, Dexter and Sheba. "Hold them as long as you can. Then head for the warehouse."

"Will do," Sheba said.

Mr. Bad hurried into the corridor. He gazed at the elevator, surprised to notice that it had stopped on the twelfth floor, then moved to the fire escape door.

"Let me go first, boss," the Claw suggested. He threw the bolt and cautiously peeked outside. "I don't see any Barons."

"Then let's split," Mr. Bad stated. He looked back once to see his lieutenants walking toward the elevator shaft, grinned, and said, "Give the bastards hell!"

Dexter and Sheba turned. Both nodded. Both watched their employer depart. And both drew M.A.C. 10's from under their jackets. Known as "the twins" by their fellow Brothers, the pair did everything together. Worked together. Ate together. Some claimed they even showered together. Now, together, they advanced to the elevator and pointed their auto pistols at the door.

"When they open the door," Dexter said.

"We'll waste them," Sheba concluded.

The indicator light over the door rose to the thirteenth floor and continued to the fourteenth.

"Ready?" Dexter asked.

"Ready," Sheba replied.

A second later the elevator whined to a halt and the door began to hiss open.

"Now!" Dexter barked.

Both men cut loose at point-blank range.

CHAPTER THIRTEEN

"Come in, my dear."

The booming voice beckoned from an immense man who was sitting behind a desk on the far side of the enormous, luxurious room, and Raphaela walked nervously forward, glancing at the half-dozen other men who were standing at various points to her right and left.

"You have nothing to be afraid of, Ms. Mundy," the man at the desk assured her. "You're a guest in my house until this unfortunate affair is concluded."

Raphaela licked her dry lips and squared her slim shoulders. The ride to the mysterious mansion had been a harrowing ordeal, what with a gun barrel pressed against her abdomen the entire trip. To compound her misery, she had seen Lobo sprawled on top of the table, and was positive that he had died while trying to protect her. Now she felt a swell of anger at these strange men who had so callously abducted her, and she focused her resentment on the huge man who appeared to be the leader of the operation. "Why does everyone keep calling me that?"

"Calling you what?" the man responded quizzically.

"Mundy."

"Because that's your name," the leader said patronizingly. "Just like mine is Arthur Owsley." He motioned at one of the chairs. "Why don't you take a seat?"

Her eyes constantly roving from man to man, Raphaela sat down and carefully deposited her hands in her lap. She was acutely conscious of the figure she must present in her skintight gown, and she wished she had never bought the thing. How could she hope to make a bid for freedom when she couldn't run very fast or even raise her leg to deliver an effective kick? She stared at her captor. "Your name may be Owsley, but mine isn't Mundy."

The leader smirked. "It's not?"

"No, it isn't."

"Your assertion is most puzzling," Owsley said. "Here you claim not to be Gloria Mundy, and yet you have red hair just like she does, green eyes just like she does, and if I may take a liberty, the same ravishing form as her." He snickered. "How, then, can you claim not to be the lady in question?"

"Easy. I'm not the woman you wanted."

"I can readily appreciate your reluctance to disclose your true identity," Owsley commented. "You undoubtedly fear for your life. Well, permit me to set your fears at rest. I know you are Mr. Bad's woman. I know you are a minor pawn in the general scheme of things. Why, you're not even an official member of the Brothers. So killing you would be a waste of my time and your beauty."

Raphaela said nothing. She hoped to learn as much as she could about the reason for her kidnapping.

"You see, my raid on the China White had a dual purpose. I hoped to catch Mr. Bad off guard while most of his men were out scouring Los Angeles for Fayanne—a ploy I masterminded, by the way. Failing to snuff him, I hoped to further embarrass the bastard by taking his woman right out from under his nose. Now I can count two coups in one week. When his people learn about your abduction, coming so soon on the heels of my triumph in obtaining his personal books, they'll desert Keif's sinking ship in droves." He smiled smugly. "There. Now that you understand, what do you think?"

"I think you're making a big mistake. When Blade learns you've taken me and killed Lobo, no one will be able to stop him."

"Blade? Who is this Blade? Why does the name sound vaguely familiar?"

"Ever heard about the Force?"

Owsley's eyes narrowed. "I've read about the Force in the paper. Blade is their leader, correct?"

"Yep."

"And what does this superman I keep reading so much about have to do with you?"

"I'm also on the Force."

Arthur Owsley and his henchmen burst into unrestrained laughter, venting their mirth for over a minute.

Raphaela waited patiently for them to stop, her cheeks crimson with indignation.

"Oh, that was priceless," Owsley stated at last, and touched the corners of his eyes. "I had no idea you possessed such a refined sense of humor."

"You won't find this situation so funny when Blade and the rest of the Force show up at your front door."

"Please, Ms. Mundy. Enough is enough. Why go to such an extreme to convince us you're a member of the Freedom Force when we both know it's patently ridiculous?"

"Don't say I didn't warn you."

Owsley leaned back and flexed his pudgy fingers. "Your stay here will be, I hope, relatively short. The Barons are looking for Mr. Bad even as we speak. His own people are scattered over south L.A., and it's only a matter of time before we nail him and end this war. Then I, Arthur Owsley, will be the reigning drug lord in L.A. My criminal empire will enable me to rule this city from behind the scenes, as it were. And who knows? From L.A. we can spread throughout the State, even establish chapters in the Civilized Zone and elsewhere."

"You're awful fond of yourself, aren't you?"

"I have every right to be," Owsley stated.

Raphaela reflected on her predicament. Now she knew her kidnappers were the Barons, one of the gangs the trooper had told her about. Somehow, she had wound up in the middle of their gang war. It must have been a simple case of being in the wrong place at the wrong time. That, and resembling the Mundy woman. It figured. Her luck was running true to form. She looked to her left as a stocky Baron stepped with obvious trepidation toward the desk.

"Uhhhh, Boss?" the Baron said.

"What is it, Barney?" Owsley asked with an air of annoyance.

"There's something I think you should know."

"First let me congratulate you on a job well done. You directed the raid on the China White admirably, even if the casualty count was higher than I anticipated would be the case."

Barney coughed lightly. "That's what I want to talk to you about."

"Elaborate."

"The boys who got racked at the club . . ." Barney began, then hesitated, his gaze averted.

"What about them?" Owsley demanded impatiently.

"Not them so much as the ones who offed our boys," Barney went on. "I've been thinking about what this dame just told us, about being on the Force and all."

Owsley laughed. "Surely even *you* don't attach any credence to her story."

Barney glanced at the redhead. "I don't know nothing about no credence, but I did read the paper about the Force outfit and what they did down in Mexico."

"So?"

"So the paper said there's a new Force. A bunch of the others got killed."

"Everyone in California knows that," Owsley stated testily. "Get to the point."

"Well, the paper said the new Force includes a redhead, an Indian, some kind of cowboy-type, a black dude, a soldier, and one of those mutation things that looks like a cat."

Owsley sighed and looked at Raphaela. "Do you see the caliber of my personnel? He beats around the bush until he's worn a rut in the ground." His hooded eyes fixed on Barney. "You have exactly ten seconds to explain the significance of your rambling."

Barney looked as if he wanted to crawl under the desk. "Well, I saw the guys who wasted our boys. One of them was a cowboy-type dressed in black, another was an Indian, and there was also some kind of cat-man."

Raphaela nearly giggled at the stupefied expression on the leader's face. He blinked a few times and gazed at her, then at the Baron called Barney.

"Why wasn't I informed of this sooner?"

Barney shrugged. "We've only been back a few minutes. And I didn't figure it was all that important. I just thought they were customers, you know?"

"Customers?" Owsley repeated softly. He abruptly rose from his chair, displaying surprising swiftness for a man with such a tremendous bulk, and glared at his lieutenant. "Customers!" he roared. "How many hybrids do you think there are in L.A.? How many Flathead Indians? How many Cavalrymen?"

"I don't know, Boss."

Owsley leaned on the desk, his visage livid. "I'll tell you, you boob! *None,* except for the members of the Force! Do you mean to tell me that the three you mentioned attacked you after you snatched this woman?"

"Yeah. And there was a big blond guy with them too, sort of a military type, if you know what I mean."

Owsley's chin sagged to his chest. "What are the odds?" he asked, apparently addressing the question to himself. "What are the *odds*?"

"Oh, yeah," Barney added. "And there was this black dude who tried to save the skirt. We offed him."

"I'm surrounded by incompetents," Owsley mumbled. His head snapped up. "You *killed* one of the Force?"

"We didn't know who he was," Barney said defensively. "We assumed he was one of the Brothers."

"You *assumed*?" Owsley bellowed, and swung toward his

prisoner. "You mentioned his name was Lobo?"

Raphaela nodded. "He was from the Clan."

"And you are—?"

"I'm a Mole. My name is Raphaela."

Owsley straightened and came slowly around the table, halting next to the stocky Baron. "Dear God, it's true! We've kidnapped one of the Force!"

"It's no big deal, Boss," Barney said. "They don't know who we are and they have no way of finding us."

Owsley's lips compressed for a moment. He glanced at another Baron. "Bennie, you're now my second-in-command."

"Bennie!" Barney exclaimed. "What about me?"

Owsley smiled, a peculiarly sinister indication of his innermost feelings. "You?" he said contemptuously. "You're history."

Raphaela was startled by the suddenness of Barney's demise. She jumped in her chair when Arthur Owsley's thick right hand, held flat and straight, swept around, up, and in, spearing into Barney's throat and crushing it.

Barney gagged and tottered backwards, clutching at his ravaged trachea, blood dribbling from the corners of his mouth. He tried to breathe, gasping loudly, and fell to his knees.

"Your incompetence has jeopardized our entire operation," Owsley said icily, advancing on the helpless Baron. "Now I must take emergency remedial measures to compensate for your stupidity." He halted, not an inch from Barney, and placed a hand on each side of Barney's head. "You've let me down, dearest Barney. Give my regards to eternity."

Raphaela saw Owsley's massive arms wrench to the right, then the left, and she distinctly heard the crackle of Barney's spine being severed. She recoiled in disgust and gripped her chair for support.

Owsley allowed the body to fall to the carpet. "Bennie, get this garbage out of my sight."

"Right away, Boss," the new second-in-command said dutifully, and gestured at two other Barons. They took hold of Barney and hoisted him into the air, then hastily exited.

"Now then," Owsley said, turning to the Molewoman, "to cases." He stepped to her left side. "You say that Blade won't rest until he has found you?"

Raphaela nodded defiantly. Although she was terrified of the psychopath, she refused to give him the satisfaction of seeing her cringe in fear. She looked him in the eye, keeping her chin firm and proud.

"And the other Force members will undoubtedly accompany him," Owsley said, more to himself than to her.

"They'll tear this place apart," Raphaela predicted.

"No, my dear. They'll try. There's a difference," Arthur Owsley said. "I have fifteen soldiers on the premises, all well-armed. They know every bush on the grounds. I'd say that the Force will be at a disadvantage should they attempt a rescue."

"You won't stop them."

"Perhaps I won't have to stop them," Owsley responded thoughtfully. He leaned against the desk and folded his arms across his chest. "What would you say to a deal?"

"A deal?"

"Yes. I'll give you your freedom in exchange for your word that you'll persuade Blade and company to refrain from coming after the Barons."

"You'll just let me walk out the front door?"

Owsley nodded.

"What's the catch?"

"There's no catch," Owsley said, and regarded her intently. "But tell me. What kind of man is this Blade? Is he everything the papers claim?"

"He's more."

"Then it doesn't matter whether you give your word or not," Owsley stated regretfully. "Such a man would never permit the death of one of his own to go unpunished. Even if we released you, he'd still hunt us down."

Raphaela did not bother to reply. Thanks to the newspaper articles, Owsley had formulated a fair estimation of the Warrior's character. If she lied, he'd know right away. "You could always turn yourself in."

"Are you serious?"

"Sure. You know what will happen if you don't. Why not surrender to the authorities and end all the bloodshed."

Owsley sighed. "If only it were that easy." He shook his head. "No, my only recourse is to prepare a lethal reception for your companions."

"What about me?"

"You'll be placed under guard in one of the upstairs bedrooms, where you should be safe."

"You're not going to kill me?" Raphaela asked, incredulous.

"Why should I? You're here by accident. You've done me no harm. Besides, I might be able to use you as a bargaining chip later," Owsley informed her, then grinned. "And who knows? If we dispose of your friends, I may just keep you for myself. It's been a while since I had a woman, and that dress of yours does wonders for your natural charms."

Raphaela tried to sink into her chair, mentally pledging never to wear a gown or dress again for as long as she lived.

"Yes, indeed," Owsley said, and licked his lips. "This could be the start of a marvelous relationship."

CHAPTER FOURTEEN

The scene at the China White resembled a madhouse. There were police cars and other official vehicles everywhere, their red lights flashing. The L.A. Police Department had established a cordon to keep out the curious. There were a half-dozen reporters already present, held at bay by two hefty officers, clamoring for answers to the questions they shouted at the man overseeing the operation, Captain Clint Callahan.

A 25-year veteran of the L.A.P.D., Callahan worked as the Chief of Detectives. He was of average height and build, with brown hair and brown eyes, and his strongest trait was his keen mind. Through long years of experience he had inured himself to the grisly sight of murder victims, or so he'd believed until he'd set foot inside the nightclub and seen the dozens of dead and dying lying in spreading pools of blood, some with their faces partly blown away, others nearly torn in half by a shotgun blast. After issuing orders, he had ventured out to the steps to inhale the cool air and collect his thoughts. He glanced distastefully at the obnoxious reporters, who he could not help but compare to a pack of braying hyenas, and was about to turn and reenter the club when he heard his name shouted and spied a patrolman hurrying toward him.

Another man accompanied the patrolman, a giant wearing a black leather vest and green fatigue pants.

Callahan studied this newcomer, and immediately detected the bulge of hidden weapons. Prudently, he kept his right hand next to the open flap of his jacket, within easy reach of his service revolver. "Yes?" he responded.

The youthful patrolman hurried up the steps and held out an identification card. "Sir, this man claims he needs to see you. I know the rule about letting civilians cross our lines, but you should take a look at his I.D."

Callahan complied, his eyes narrowing when he read the name of the man to whom it belonged and saw the governor's signature in the lower right corner. He looked at the giant, who had halted three steps below. "So you're Blade?"

The Warrior simply nodded.

"That will be all," Callahan said to the patrolman, who eagerly retraced his route. "What can I do for you?"

Blade nodded at the entrance. "I have reason to believe my team was here earlier."

"The Force? Here?" Callahan declared in surprise.

"Governor Melnick offered us three days off in L.A.," Blade explained. "My unit came here for some relaxation."

"And that's all?" Callahan asked, a tinge of suspicion to his tone.

"Why else?"

"You tell me."

Blade returned the police officer's steady gaze. "I don't know what you're talking about. I'd like to go inside, if you don't mind?"

Callahan pondered for a moment. "No, I don't mind. But be sure and tell the governor I'm such a nice guy so I can rack up some Brownie points."

"I will," Blade said, puzzled by the police officer's sarcastic tone. "Who are you?"

"Sorry. Captain Callahan, Chief of Detectives."

"Pleased to meet you," Blade remarked, and offered his right hand.

Callahan relaxed somewhat and shook, impressed by the controlled strength in the giant's grip. "So how come you weren't with your unit?"

"I had paperwork to catch up on."

"Say no more," Callahan said. "I know what you mean. I hate the damn stuff myself."

Blade glanced at the doorway. "What happened in there?"

"Come with me," Callahan directed, and led the way indoors. He surreptitiously scrutinized the giant as they walked, gauging the truthfulness of the Warrior's answers and reactions. "Do you know whose club this is?"

"No."

"Really? Well, it belongs to the Brothers. Mr. Bad runs it personally."

"Mr. Bad? The Brothers?"

"You don't know about the Brothers, one of the leading gangs in the city?"

Blade shook his head.

"Then let me enlighten you," Callahan said. "There are two gangs fighting for control of L.A. One is known as the Brothers, the other is the Hollywood Barons. They're involved in a major war right now."

"And you suspect the Barons hit this nightclub?"

"I do."

Worry lines appeared on the Warrior's face. "How many were killed?"

"We're still tallying the list," Callahan said. "So far, we have twenty-six stiffs in body bags."

"Were any of them from the Force?" Blade asked anxiously, his concerned gaze on the end of the hallway.

"Not that I'm aware of," Callahan responded. "We haven't found any with a Force I.D."

Blade expelled a breath in relief. If anything happened to them, he would hold himself accountable. He should have been with his team, not sulking at the compound. Except for Havoc, they had no idea what to expect in a big city.

"The hit doesn't make much sense, though," Callahan mentioned. "As near as we can determine, there were no Brothers killed, just innocent bystanders. It's almost as if the Barons blew away the bystanders to keep anyone from interfering with their real purpose for attacking the club."

"Which was?"

"If I knew that, I'd be a happy man."

Blade reached the club proper and paused to survey the slaughter. He had seen worse carnage, but the sight still sickened him, and the thought of so many blameless people dying at the hands of savage, amoral butchers aroused his animosity.

"Did you have any idea this place was going to be hit?" Callahan inquired.

Blade glanced at the detective in surprise. "No. How would I know?"

Callahan smiled. "Just asking."

A tall, dark-haired man wearing a brown trench coat approached, a small notepad in his left hand.

"What have we got, Harry?" Callahan inquired.

The man stopped, gave the Warrior a curious appraisal, then consulted his notes. "Just a rough sketch, so far, but from what the witnesses tell us it all started when a group of men, reports vary from seven to fifteen, came through the door in the southeast corner and began firing at random."

"The bastards," Callahan interrupted passionately.

"Yeah. Anyway, from there on out it gets real confusing. There are some reports that gunshots were exchanged, that a guy in a black cowboy outfit shot several of the attackers. We've checked for tattoos, and we've confirmed there were seven Barons killed."

"There were?"

"Yep. Someone, probably the Brothers, collected all the weapons before we arrived, so we had no way of telling if any of the dead were gang members until we verified they wore tattoos."

"I understand."

"Well, out of the seven Barons killed, four were shot, two had their throats torn to shreds, and one was knifed," Harry detailed. "Oh, yeah. And we just found a pair of dead Brothers out back."

"And they're the only dead Brothers on the premises?"

"They're all we'e found."

"Excellent. Keep me informed."

Harry hefted the notepad. "That's not all, Clint."

"What else?"

"Several of the witnesses claim that the two Barons who had their necks ripped open were attacked by a cat-man, a hybrid."

"Oh?" Callahan responded, and regarded the giant coldly.

"Yep. They also claim an Indian was involved. But here's the main item. Every witness agrees that the Brothers didn't put up much of a fight. There must not have been the usual number of Brothers at the club tonight."

"Interesting."

"And so is this. We have customers who say that the Barons kidnapped a woman."

"Any idea who she could be?"

"Not yet. The descriptions are all the same. A redheaded fox in a blue gown."

Blade's interest flared. "Redhead? Did you say redhead?"

"That's what they claim," Harry replied.

"Why is her hair color significant?" Callahan inquired.

"One of the Force is a redhead. Raphaela, the volunteer from the Moles," Blade disclosed.

"Do tell," Callahan said.

"But why would the Barons take Raphaela?" Blade wondered aloud.

"I'm hoping you can tell me," Callahan stated.

"I have no idea," Blade said softly, his emotions in turmoil. Raphaela had been captured by the Barons! His team had become embroiled in a gang war! How? Why? They had been on their own for only a few hours, and already they were up to their necks in serious trouble. He had to find them, to rescue Raphaela. "Where could I find the Barons?" he asked gruffly.

"We don't know where they have their base of operations," Callahan answered before Harry could reply.

"Who *would* know?"

"Mr. Bad might."

"And where would I find him?"

"He has a condo on Westminster Avenue. The Sorel Manor, they call the place. Seventy-five Westminster. You can't miss it."

Blade smiled at the detective. "Thanks. I owe you one." He wheeled and stalked from the nightclub.

"Did I miss something here?" Harry asked when the giant had disappeared through the doorway.

"Yep," Callahan said, and cackled.

"We know where the Barons are based," Harry noted. "It's no secret that Arthur Owsley is their head, and his mansion is at Twelve Hundred Sunset Boulevard in West Hollywood."

"I know," Callahan stated, and snickered in triumph.

"Then why did you lie to that guy?"

"Do you know who he was?"

"You didn't introduce me."

"Forgive my deplorable manners," Callahan quipped. "That was Blade."

"*The* Blade? The head honcho of the Force?"

Callahan nodded. "The one and only."

"Why would you lie to him? I thought he's a good guy."

"He lied to me so I returned the favor."

Harry scratched his head. "You've lost me, Clint."

"That cowboy and the cat-man those witnesses saw are members of the Force, just like the redhead who was abducted. I asked Blade what his team was doing here, and he had the gall to tell me they were on the town or some such bullshit. I don't buy it for a minute."

"You don't?"

"Hell, no. Here we have the Brothers and the Barons involved in a full-scale war, and the Force just *happens* to get entangled in the whole mess? Give me a break. That's too much of a coincidence for me to swallow."

"Then what's going down?"

Callahan smirked. "Our illustrious governor is pulling another of his brilliant political moves."

"Huh?"

"Haven't you noticed how Governor Melnick milks the Force for every vote he can get? Well, he's decided to sic his elite band of assassins on the Brothers and the Barons. He's aware of all the headlines since the gang war erupted. He's probably fed up with all the negative news and the repercussions for his administration. So he's sent in the Force on the sly to destroy both gangs." Callahan snickered. "The man is a wizard."

"I still don't understand why you lied to Blade," Harry remarked.

"He probably already knows all about Owsley. Even if he doesn't, I'm killing two birds with one stone. For years we've been trying to slam the lid on Owsley and Keif, but their high-priced lawyers always get them off the hook. And we're virtually helpless because we have to go by the book. We have to stick to the letter of the law," Callahan said, and nodded toward the entrance. "Blade is under no such constraints. His allegiance is to the Federation as a whole, and he has authorization to do whatever is necessary to secure the safety of any faction."

"Meaning?"

"Meaning that big son of a bitch can kick ass any way he wants, and the law be damned. He can take out both Owsley and Keif and there's not a damn thing anyone can do or say about it," Callahan said, and laughed. "That Melnick is brilliant. He's provided the Force with the perfect cover story. They can claim they were out on the town when they were attacked by one of the gangs. No one will know any different. Everyone will hail them as heroes and Governor Melnick will get the vote of everybody in L.A. for cleaning up the slime."

"Wow," Harry declared in appreciation. "You're right. Their plan is ingenious."

"Blade and the Force will take care of the Brothers and the Barons, and we don't have to lift a finger to help them."

Harry stared at his superior. "How in the world did you ever figure this all out? I never would've made the connection."

Callahan stood a little straighter. "When you've been a detective as long as I have, you develop a nose for these things."

"My compliments."

"Thanks. Now get your ass in gear."

"Beg pardon?"

"None of the higher-ups saw fit to tell us about this operation, but now that we know I'm not about to be left in the dark. I want you to follow Blade. Wherever he goes, you go. Phone in every chance you get and keep me informed on his activities."

Harry nodded and started to run for the door.

"And Harry?"

The detective paused. "Yeah?"

"Under no circumstances are you to interfere with Blade or the Force, and don't let anyone else interfere either. If anyone gives you any grief, have them call me."

"Will do," Harry said, and raced off.

Captain Callahan rubbed his hands together and beamed. This was a dream come true! The lousy Barons and Brothers wiped out in one fell swoop, and all he had to do was sit on his tush until it was all over and clean up the mess.

Christmas in August!

CHAPTER FIFTEEN

Dexter and Sheba emptied half their magazines into the elevator, their M.A.C. 10's chattering metallically, before they realized there was no one inside. They ceased firing simultaneously and glanced at one another.

"Where the hell are the Barons?" Dexter snapped.

"Maybe we were mistaken," Sheba said. "Maybe the Barons weren't attacking."

"Then what was that noise we heard that sounded like an explosion?" Dexter countered, and moved warily forward, sweeping his M.A.C. 10 from side to side.

"Mr. Bad will be ticked off if he finds out he split for no reason," Sheba predicted.

"This is fishy," Dexter said. He entered the elevator and stared at the bullet holes in the walls, then at the control panel situated to the left of the door. Elevators didn't operate by themselves. *Someone* had sent the car to the top floor. But who? And why send it up empty? If the Barons were up to no good, what purpose did it serve? It wasn't as if the sons of bitches could hide in it. Not unless they opened the maintenance panel on the roof and hid on top of the . . .

The maintenance panel!

Dexter pivoted and tried to bring his M.A.C. 10 to bear on the ceiling, but he was too late. He saw a furry form crouched in the opening, and then a thin form pounced on his chest and bore him to the floor. Claws or nails gouged into his neck and he released the M.A.C. 10 to grab his assailant.

Shocked by the abrupt assault, Sheba took several strides forward, trying to get a bead on the figure battling Dexter, but they were rolling and thrashing, turning and twisting, and he was afraid to fire for fear of hitting his companion. He glimpsed the fur and the fangs of the feline features on the creature and realized Dexter had been jumped by a mutation. So concerned was he for Dexter's safety, he failed to take into account his own.

Dexter and the hybrid rolled from the elevator, still fighting, crimson coating Dexter's neck.

"Get clear!" Sheba urged frantically, flattening against the right wall so they could pass him by. He heard a thump from the elevator and started to rotate, astonished to see an Indian springing at him, the same Indian who had shown up at the China White earlier. He swung the M.A.C. 10, but the Indian blocked it with his left palm, then delivered a stunning right to Sheba's jaw. The next instant the Indian closed in, and they grappled and fell to the red carpet.

No slouch at hand-to-hand combat, Sheba let go of the M.A.C. 10 and tried to lance his fingers into the Indian's eyes at the same moment he drove his left knee at the other man's crotch. To his consternation, both blows were deflected, and then the Indian had him in a headlock and hard knuckles were digging into the base of his throat and restricting his ability to breathe.

"Lie still or I'll break your neck!" the Indian warned.

Sheba resisted for a few more seconds, just long enough to satisfy himself he couldn't break the headlock without a supreme effort, and that in that time his adversary would undoubtedly fulfill the threat.

Footsteps pounded in the corridor.

From his position lying flat on his back with the Indian on top, Sheba looked up to behold three men appear, three more who had been to the club. He saw the cowboy, the loud-mouthed guy in the leather jacket who now sported a crude white bandage on his head, and the blond. The cowboy held a revolver, while the latter two had picked up the discarded M.A.C. 10's.

"Good job, Sparrow," the blond said.

"Thank you, Havoc," the Indian responded, and unexpectedly stood, drawing a hunting knife as he rose.

Sheba suddenly found every weapon trained on him, and he coughed and rose slowly onto his elbows. "I give up," he declared. "Don't kill me."

"Where's Mr. Bad?" Havoc asked.

"I don't know," Sheba lied. "He cut out after we heard an explosion downstairs."

"He must've gone down the fire escape," the injured guy said, and ran toward the end of the corridor.

"Be careful, Lobo," Havoc advised. "Doc, you go with him."

The cowboy in black departed.

"Can I get up?" Sheba queried.

"Be my guest," Havoc responded.

His bruised throat aching terribly, Sheba rose. "Where's Dex—?" he began, turning to the left, the word dying on his lips as he laid eyes on the blood-splattered form of his friend lying six feet away. Dexter's neck had been torn to shredded ribbons and his mouth hung open. "No!"

The furry figure crouched next to Dexter slowly unfurled to his full height and turned, his hands held near his waist, blood dripping from his nails. His slanted eyes focused on Sheba. "Do you want me to dispose of this one too?"

"Not yet, Jag," Havoc responded, scanning the corridor. Lobo and Doc were almost to the fire escape. Much closer were two doors, a closed red one and a brown door that stood ajar. "Keep an eye on him while Sparrow and I check out the condo."

"My pleasure," Jag said, and deliberately grinned to expose his pointed teeth.

Sheba flinched as if struck. "Hey, man," he said to Havoc. "You can't leave me alone with this . . . *thing*!"

"Watch me," Havoc retorted, and headed for the open door, the M.A.C. 10 gripped in both hands. He swung his back to the wall and cautiously stepped to the jamb, then quickly glanced within. There was no one in sight, but he could hear a faint noise, the clink of ice in a glass. Puzzled, he pushed the door with his right foot and leaped into the condo, staying doubled over at the waist, Sparrow on his heels. He darted forward into a living room and halted abruptly when he saw the lovely redheaded woman in a yellow gown sitting on a sofa, a large glass in her right hand.

"Hi, there, handsome," the woman said cheerily, and took a healthy swallow of her drink. She lowered the glass and giggled. "Don't mind me, honey. I'm trying to get plastered to the gills."

Mystified by her indifferent attitude to their arrival, Havoc straightened and surveyed the rest of the condo, noting there were other doors. "What's your name?"

"Mundy, handsome. Gloria Mundy," she said, and tipped her glass again.

"Is anyone else here?"

"Nope. Just little old me," Gloria replied, and giggled.

Havoc glanced at the Flathead. "Check anyway."

Nodding, Sparrow moved toward the doors.

"Don't you believe me?" Gloria queried, sounding hurt. "What is this? Dump-on-Mundy night or something?"

"I can't take any chances," Havoc told her. "This is Mr. Bad's condo, isn't it?"

"Yeah," Gloria said, her mouth curling downward. "The prick lives here."

"And what about the other one across the hall, the one with the red door?"

"That's my place, or it used to be. I've taken all the abuse I'm going to take from that son of a bitch. I plan to pack up and haul ass," Gloria stated angrily, and took yet another gulp.

"Was Mr. Bad here?"

"Yeah. He cut out a bit ago, him and that freaky bodyguard of his, the Claw." Gloria shuddered and drank some more, then smacked her red lips. "I never knew straight whiskey could taste so good."

"Do you happen to know the address of the Barons' mansion?" Havoc inquired.

"The Barons? Nope. Sure don't," Gloria answered, slurring her words a tad. She tittered. "Hey, there's an idea. Maybe I'll find out and go offer my bod to Owsley. I bet he likes a good lay as much as the next guy. And I'm a *good* lay!"

"I'll bet," Havoc muttered, and saw Sparrow return. "Anything?"

"Empty."

"Okay," Havoc said. He turned toward the corridor and raised his voice. "Jag, bring that joker in here."

Gloria Mundy winked at Sparrow Hawk. "Hey, there, sailor."

"I'm an Indian."

"I can see you are, cutie-pie. I've never had an Indian before. What are you like in the sack?"

"I sometimes snore."

"Snore?" Gloria said, and cackled so hard she spilled a little of her drink. "I like a man with a sense of humor. Have you ever been around the world?"

"No," Sparrow answered. "California is the farthest I have been from my people."

It took Gloria all of 15 seconds to comprehend his reply, and then she bent in half with unrestrained mirth.

Jaguarundi entered, shoving their prisoner ahead of him. "Here's Sunshine," he quipped.

"Sheba!" Gloria Mundy exclaimed. "You look a little worse for wear, babe."

"Get stuffed, bimbo," the Brother said sullenly.

Gloria tittered. "What did I ever do to you?"

"That's enough out of both of you," Havoc said, and jerked his left thumb at the lean man in the brown suit. "This guy claims he doesn't know where Mr. Bad went. What about it, Gloria?"

"He's lying."

Sheba took a stride toward her, his fists clenched. "Shut up, you stupid bitch!"

Havoc instantly pivoted and executed the *Kinteki-seashi-geri,* kicking his right instep into the Brother's testicles. The blow made Sheba grunt and drop to his knees. Havoc whipped his left hand down, his index finger extended, delivering an *Ippon-nukite* strike to the temple, his bony finger the equivalent of a blackjack.

Stunned, Sheba sagged, his hands holding his groin.

"Hold this," Havoc said, and tossed the M.A.C. 10 to Jaguarundi, who deftly caught the weapon.

"Hit the scumbag again!" Gloria urged.

Havoc reached down, gripped the Brother's chin, and snapped the man's head up so he could glare into Sheba's eyes. "No more games, asshole. I'm tired of being treated like a lightweight. This is the Force you're dealing with, you stupid son of a bitch. If you don't give me the answers I need, Jag here will do to you what he did to your friend."

"The Force?" Sheba blurted.

"Yeah. The Freedom Force. I take it you've heard of us?"

The Brother, his eyes wide, nodded.

"Good. Then don't play around. Where did Mr. Bad and the Claw go?"

Sheba opened his mouth, then closed it.

"You asked for it, dipstick," Havoc said, straightening. "Jag, he's all yours."

The hybrid beamed and took a step forward.

"Wait!" Sheba cried, glancing nervously at the mutation. "I'll tell you what you want to know."

"I haven't got all day," Havoc snapped.

"They went to the warehouse, man."

"What warehouse?"

"Over on Warner Avenue in Santa Ana. Thirty-seven Fifty-nine Warner."

"What's there?"

"It's the warehouse where we keep our stash of weapons and where we store a lot of our big drug shipments."

"Weapons, huh?" Havoc responded thoughtfully. "One more thing. Where's the Barons' mansion located?"

"Owsley's place?"

"Do they have another mansion?"

"No. It's at Twelve Hundred Sunset Boulevard. Up in West Hollywood."

"Thank you," Havoc said politely, and snap-kicked the Brother on the jaw, causing blood to squirt from Sheba's lower lip. Without another word the man collapsed.

Jaguarundi chuckled. "I love it when you get forceful. Has anyone ever told you that you're a lot like Blade?"

The innocent query made Havoc stiffen and frown. "No," he answered testily.

"Which will we do first?" Sparrow Hawk inquired. "Go to the warehouse or go to the mansion?"

"What do you use for brains?" Jag responded. "We'll go after Raphaela first, of course."

"No, we won't," Havoc said, correcting him.

Jag did a double take. "Say again?"

"We need more weapons. Two M.A.C. 10's, the revolver, a hunting knife, and Lobo's NATO aren't enough if we're going to attack the Barons in their own stronghold. I say we go to the warehouse first and obtain the weapons we need," Havoc explained.

"Your proposal sounds wise," Sparrow said.

"I don't know," Jag said. "What about Raphaela?"

"What about her? What good would it do her for us to assault the mansion if the Barons have superior firepower? Do you think they'll be using slingshots?"

"No."

"Then we need weapons," Havoc reiterated. "And there should be all the weapons we'll require at the warehouse."

"What warehouse?" a new voice interjected, and Lobo and Doc entered the condo.

The captain turned to them. "I'll explain on the way. I don't suppose you saw any sign of Mr. Bad?"

"Nope," Lobo said. "We went all the way to the bottom. He's long gone."

"But we know where to find him," Havoc informed them.

"What about this trash?" Jag inquired, pointing at Sheba.

"Tie him up but good. We'll leave him here and phone

the police later."

Jag walked to the right wall, picked up a lamp, and tore the electrical cord off the base with a yank of his powerful sinews.

"What about me, lover?" Gloria Mundy spoke up.

"You can do whatever you want," Havoc replied.

"Goody. I think I'll help myself to a few more drinks before I take off."

"Let's go find a cab," Havoc stated to the others.

"You don't need a cab," Gloria declared.

"We don't?"

"Nope. Look in Sheba's front pockets. You should find a key to a green Chevy parked in the lot out back."

Havoc smiled. "Thanks."

"No problem," Gloria said. "But there is a favor I'd like you to do."

"What?"

"When you finally catch up with Mr. Bad, give the bum one of those fancy kicks for me."

"It'll be my pleasure."

CHAPTER SIXTEEN

Raphaela sat on the edge of the bed in a room on the second floor of Arthur Owsley's mansion, her expression glum, and stared at the two Barons who had been assigned to guard her. They were standing near one of the windows fronting the south side of the mansion, their arms folded, conversing in muted tones. Each man had an AK-47 slung over his left shoulder.

What should she do?

She looked down at herself, at the detestable gown, and frowned. Here was another fine mess she'd gotten herself into! And it was up to her to get herself out. She was a member of the Force, darn it all, the best combat unit on the continent. She should be able to escape without the aid of her friends.

But how?

Raphaela gazed at the closed door 12 feet to her left. There were not only guards in her room, there were Barons posted on each floor and at least a half-dozen patrolling the grounds. How could she escape when the odds were stacked against her?

"Hey, lady," one of the guards unexpectedly said. "Would you like something to drink?"

"Drink?" Raphaela repeated absently.

"Yeah. I'm going downstairs for a pop. The boss said to give you whatever you want, so do you want a drink or not?"

"A pop would be nice. Thanks."

"For a cute dish like you, anything." He smiled and left, closing the door behind him.

Raphaela studied the remaining Baron, a young man in his early twenties with sandy colored hair and blue eyes. He studiously avoided gazing in her direction. "Hi," she said.

"Hi," he mumbled while watching out the window.

"What's your name?"

"They call me Tab."

"I'm Raphaela."

"So I was told."

Raphaela scrutinized him closely, estimating they were approximately the same height and weight. His clothing particularly interested her, a beige shirt and jeans about her size. An idea occurred to her, and she decided to act before the other Baron came back. "You're not being very friendly."

"The boss told us to keep our distance or else," Tab disclosed without turning around.

"Can't you be the least bit nice? I'm scared out of my wits and I need someone to talk to."

The young Baron rotated at last and regarded her intently. "I suppose it would be okay just to talk."

Raphaela grinned and patted the bedspread beside her. "Why don't you sit over here?"

"Not on your life."

"Why not?"

"Mr. Owsley would skin me alive."

Pouting, Raphaela let her shoulders slump and bowed her head. "Oh, I understand. You don't trust me."

"It's not that," Tab said.

"Then what? You'd be doing me a favor. I'm sure Mr. Owsley wouldn't mind."

The young Baron glanced at the door, then at the bed. His eyes rested on her shoulders and the cleavage revealed by the gown. "I guess it might be okay, but just for a few minutes, until Gus gets back."

"Thank you," Raphaela said, and gave him her most radiant smile. She had never used her feminine wiles to deceive a man before, and she found the experience delightfully fascinating. Her aunt had kept her so sheltered during her teen years, a prisoner almost, that she had never dated boys her own age, never known the thrill of a romantic evening, never known the gentle touch of a man who truly cared. Her only sexual experience, if she dared call that nightmare such, hardly counted.

Tab walked over and sat down several feet from her. "What do you want to talk about?"

"Anything. How about you?"

"What about me?"

"How long have you been a Baron?"

"I don't know. Ten years maybe."

"That long?"

"Why not? I got into the gang to get the bread for my habit, and I've been going strong ever since."

"Your habit?" Raphaela questioned.

"Yeah, lady. My habit. I'm hooked on the hard stuff, you know?"

"Hard stuff?"

"Drugs, lady. Damn! Where are you from? The moon?"

Raphaela pretended to be stung by his rebuke. She averted her face and said softly, "I'm sorry I'm so ignorant. I'm from the Mound and no one there uses drugs."

Tab slid nearer. "Hey, I didn't mean anything by that remark. Really."

"That's all right. I know you're probably embarrassed talking to a dummy like me," Raphaela said sadly, her chin on her chest.

"You're not a dummy," Tab responded. "You're just upset because of everything that's happened to you." He placed his hand gently on her shoulder. "Don't worry. You'll be fine."

"I know," Raphaela stated firmly, mentally reviewing the technique Blade had taught her, hoping she could perform the move properly, tensing her right arm and holding her fingers straight and tight. Twisting, she smiled coyly at the Baron and then, when their eyes were locked, when he was totally distracted by her apparent friendliness and her physical charms, she struck. Her right arm swept out and around, her hand rigid, and she was almost as shocked as the young Baron when the edge of her hand connected with the soft flesh on his throat.

Tab gagged and tried to stand, his hands instinctively going to his neck.

Raphaela stood, brought her right arm forward, and then drove her elbow back again, planting it on the Baron's nose, breaking his nostrils and sending crimson spray shooting from his nasal passages.

Sliding frantically away from her, Tab struggled to his feet.

Raphaela spun, remembering the advice the Warrior had given her: "When in doubt, go for the gonads." She did, planting her left foot where it would do the most harm, and she was rewarded by Tab falling to his knees. He was in exquisite agony but not out yet.

Hurry! her mind shrieked.

Gus would be coming back soon!

Her anxiety mounting, Raphaela kicked him in the stomach, making him bend over. She jumped into the air and brought both her kneecaps down on the back of his head, slamming his face into the floor.

Tab went suddenly limp.

Move! Move! Move!

Squatting, Raphaela relieved the Baron of the AK-47, then began to hurriedly strip off his clothes. Fortunately he wore underwear. In less than a minute she had his jeans and shirt on the bed and was quickly removing her gown. As she peeled the garment from her like a banana skin and stood for a second in her panties and bra, she felt terribly exposed and vulnerable. Donning the jeans and the shirt took mere moments, although she had to tug to get the pants on over her combat boots.

Somewhere in the hallway a voice sounded.

Raphaela scooped up the AK-47 and moved a yard behind the door, her finger on the trigger. No sooner was she in position than the knob started to turn, and she braced herself as the door opened.

"What the hell!"

Stepping from concealment, Raphaela trained the AK-47 on Gus, who was framed in the doorway. "Quiet! Get in here!"

The Baron had a can of pop in each hand. He gawked at Tab, then glared at her. "You bitch!" he hissed.

"Quiet!" Raphaela repeated, and moved a pace closer. "Don't think I can't use this. I've been trained by the best."

His eyes pinpoints of hatred, Gus slowly elevated his arms and came into the bedroom. "And you didn't look like you could harm a flea," he muttered, watching a rivulet of blood flow from under Tab's nose.

"Never underestimate a member of the Force," Raphaela boasted. "Not put those cans and your gun on the bed. Be sure and do it very, very slowly."

Scowling, Gus obeyed her command, depositing the cans first and then carefully slipping the AK-47 from his shoulder onto the bedspread. "There, bitch. I hope you're satisfied," he snapped.

"Not quite," Raphaela responded, and moved in from the rear, her right boot lashing out and catching him behind the knee.

Taken unawares, Gus buckled.

Swinging her AK-47 in a half-circle, Raphaela slammed the Baron on the head as he went down, the heavy stock thudding against his cranium and dazing him. He landed on his left knee and attempted to right himself. "Sweet dreams," she said, and clubbed him again, then once more for good measure, and finally he pitched onto his face beside his fellow Baron.

Moving rapidly now, Raphaela went to the doorway and checked the hall, relieved to find there were no Barons in sight. She eased out and made for the stairs leading to the ground floor, hoping she could reach the front door undetected. Once outside, she could lose herself in the gardens surrounding the mansion. When only five feet from the stairs, she stopped, listening. And it was well she did.

A Baron suddenly materialized in front of her, at the top of the staircase, his head turned away from her, a shotgun in his left hand.

Raphaela reacted instantly, taking hold of the AK-47 by the barrel and swinging the weapon like a club as she charged.

The Baron heard her and tried to spin, but he was too slow.

With a pronounced thud the stock crashed into the gang member's face, full on the mouth, and the man was knocked backwards to tumble down the stairs. Raphaela stepped into the open in time to see him somersault to the bottom and wind up in a disjointed heap, apparently unconscious, the shotgun lying on the steps, about halfway down.

"What the hell was that?" someone cried.

It was now or never!

Raphaela bounded down the steps, taking three at a leap, almost losing her balance on the third one from the bottom, but she corrected her stride and came down next to the insensate Baron. The front door, if her bearings were accurate, should be to her left, and she whirled in that direction to discover a stupefied Baron not ten feet away, an M-16 cradled under his right arm.

The man tried to bring his weapon to bear.

On pure instinct, Raphaela pointed the AK-47 and squeezed the trigger, holding on tightly as the assault rifle bucked in her hands and thundered its staccato rhythm of death.

A deluge of heavy slugs tore into the Baron, perforating his torso and sending him flying. He crashed onto his back and tried feebly to rise, but couldn't.

Raphaela raced along the hall, passing the Baron and observing his eyes already beginning to glaze lifelessly. She reached the next junction, and there was the front door.

And two more Barons.

Crouching, the stock pressed against her thigh, Raphaela fired, unleashing a rain of lead that bored into the pair and drove them back against the door, blood spurting from their wounds. They started to crumple and she made for the entrance and freedom.

"Hold it!"

The bellow from her right caused her to drop and roll just as a shotgun blasted and a chunk of door exploded outward. She glanced along the right-hand corridor and spotted her foe, a skinny Baron with a ring in his nose. Before he could cut loose again, she angled the barrel and let him have a half-dozen rounds in the chest.

He screamed as he died.

There was no time to lose!

Raphaela shoved to her feet and lunged at the door, grabbing the knob and turning. Or trying to, because the front door had been locked.

NO!

She stepped back, pointing the AK-47 at the panel to blow the lock to smithereens.

"That would be naughty," said a familiar voice behind her.

Raphaela started to turn, but bands of steel seemed to enclose her body as two huge arms encircled her and held fast. She felt moist lips press against her right ear.

"Feel free to struggle, my dear. I'd enjoy that."

About to kick and thrash in an effort to bust loose, Raphaela relaxed instead, willing herself to stay calm, not to lose control. "Forget it, Owsley," she said. "I won't give you the satisfaction."

"Perhaps not now, but later you will," the head Baron predicted. "Kindly drop your weapon."

Reluctant to give up, Raphaela hesitated.

Owsley tightened his enormous arms, displaying his prodigious strength, revealing that every square inch of him was hardened muscle.

Raphaela gasped as the constriction on her chest resulted in intense pain and discomfort. Those arms of his were like pythons. She let go of the AK-47 and the gun clattered at her feet.

"How obliging of you," Owsley said. He suddenly slackened his grasp and gave her a shove, sending her sprawling into the front door. In a flash he retrieved the AK-47.

Barely catching herself in time to prevent her forehead from bashing the wooden door panel, Raphaela pivoted.

"Please don't be foolhardy," Owsley advised, his tone acidic. "I may want to trifle with you later, but that won't stop me from killing you now if you cause more trouble."

Other Barons appeared, converging from every direction.

"Gus and Tab are out cold upstairs," one of the gang members reported. "And Eddie is at the bottom of the stairs. He'll live, but his face will never be the same."

Owsley gazed at the two bodies near the door, the dead shotgun-wielder, and then at the first man she had killed farther down the hall. His lips curved downward. "Four dead and three injured. You are far more formidable than I believed." He sighed. "Very well. I shall *personally* escort you back to the bedroom and *personally* bind you so that you can't move more than your eyelids, and then we shall wait for your friends from the Force to arrive."

"They'll be here," Raphaela said defiantly.

"I hope they come soon," Owsley responded. "I can't wait to finish with them so I can repay you for all the aggravation you've caused me." He leered at her. "Three guesses what I have in mind."

CHAPTER SEVENTEEN

Gloria Mundy was having the time of her life.

She alternated her time between drinking, singing to herself, drinking, walking over to kick Sheba every now and then, drinking, and cursing Haywood Keif from the comfort of his sofa.

Right now she was taking another sip of whiskey while sneering at Sheba, who had been bent into the shape of a pretzel and bound securely and gagged by the hybrid. The Brother had regained consciousness 15 minutes ago. He was lying near the bar, facing her, glaring and uttering incomprehensible oaths through the dirty sock the hybrid had crammed into his mouth.

"What's that?" Gloria asked. "You'll have to speak up. I can't hear you." She threw back her head and laughed, rating herself as the funniest person on the planet.

Sheba voiced inarticulate growls and grunts and struggled in vain against the electrical cord binding his wrists and ankles.

Gloria leaned forward. "Did you say you have to take a

leak? Sorry, asshole. Go in your pants."

His features beet red, Sheba bucked and heaved to no avail.

"I wish I had a camera," Gloria joked, and swallowed more whiskey. Her senses were swimming and she had difficulty focusing, but she didn't care. She was feeling no pain, and that was how she wanted to feel.

Sheba ceased his struggles and rested his forehead on the floor.

"Are you done with the temper tantrum?" Gloria queried sarcastically.

The Brother could only glower.

"How does that sock taste?" Gloria wondered. "I told that cat-guy where to find Mr. Bad's clothes hamper. Aren't I a peach?"

Sheba renewed his futile efforts to free himself.

Gloria suddenly realized her glass was empty. "Damn! How did this happen?" She stood and walked unsteadily over to the bar, pausing to give Sheba a healthy jab in the ribs with her left foot. He went insane, bouncing and rolling about like a fish out of water. "Boy, some people are real grumps," she said, and tittered.

Sheba abruptly stopped, his body aligned in the direction of the front door, his eyes almost bulging from their sockets.

"That's better," Gloria chided him. "You have pitiful manners." She grabbed the whiskey bottle and upended it into her glass, frowning when the bottle went dry after giving her only half a refill. "Will you look at this? We're running low on happy juice."

The Brother did not even bother to grunt. He seemed to be trying to sink out of sight in the carpet.

"What's the matter, honey?" Gloria asked. "Dirty sock got your tongue?" She cackled and turned to retrace her steps to the sofa.

And saw *him*.

"Dear God!" she blurted out, amazed by the gigantic figure standing not five feet away, a veritable colossus whose muscles appeared to have been sculpted from bronzed marble. She inadvertently let go of her glass and felt the whiskey splash her feet and legs. "Who the hell are you?"

"I'll ask the questions," the giant informed her.

"Whatever you say. I make it a point never to argue with a guy the size of King Kong."

"King who?"

"You know," Gloria said. "That big, hairy gorilla who goes around feeling up the broads."

The giant stared at her strangely for a few seconds, as if he couldn't decide if she was serious or not. He watched her sway from side to side and sniffed the air. "You're inebriated."

Gloria stuck her nose in the air and held her shoulders steady. "I am not, and I resent your insenu—insinula—what you said."

"Is this Mr. Bad's condo?"

"Sure is. Or was," Gloria replied, and snickered.

"He's not here?"

"Nope. Flew the coop."

Pursing his lips, the giant looked down at Sheba. "Who's this?"

"His name is Shit-for-Brains," Gloria answered.

The giant placed his hands on his hips, next to two bulges under his black leather vest. "Do you happen to know the Barons?"

"Not personally. Yet."

"Then you wouldn't know where their base of operations is located?"

"Their base?" Gloria said, perplexed, her brow furrowed. "Oh! You mean Owsley's mansion."

"Owsley?"

"Yep. Arthur Owsley. The leader of the Barons," Gloria disclosed. She glanced at Sheba. "And yeah, I do happen to know the address."

The giant loomed above her before she could take another breath, his visage a mask of strained intensity, and the next words he spoke were low and grating. "What is it?"

Gloria stared up into his piercing gray eyes and shivered. "The mansion is in West Hollywood. Twelve Hundred Sunset Boulevard."

He whirled and departed without another word, vanishing

out the front door as insubstantially as a ghost, making no sound, saying nothing more.

Blinking in bewilderment, Gloria gazed at the doorway and wondered if she had imagined the whole thing. She pondered the giant's interest in the Barons, and after a minute her sluggish mind came to a conclusion and she frowned. "Damn. So much for trying to bed Owsley." She glanced down at Sheba. "I guess the Barons can kiss their asses goodbye, huh?"

The Brother simply glared at her.

"You know something?" Gloria snapped. "You're rude." So saying, and just for the general hell of it, she kicked him in the head.

CHAPTER EIGHTEEN

"We'll drive around the block one more time," Havoc proposed, and took a left at the corner, keeping his eyes on the warehouse.

Three stories in height and 50 yards in length, the exterior of the building had been painted a dull brown many years ago. The paint was now peeling, and the entire warehouse had been neglected to the point where the structure badly needed repairs. Several of the upper windows were cracked or had panes missing. The windows on the ground floor, though, were all intact and barred. On the west side a single door was located under a faded sign bearing the word OFFICE in large black letters. To the east a loading dock, bordered by a parking lot, ran almost the width of the warehouse. A towering corrugated metal door served as the entryway for the goods unloaded on the dock.

"It ain't going to be easy gettin' in there," Lobo commented.

"We've got to find a way," Doc said. "I don't like the idea of coming here while Raphaela is in the hands of those lowlifes."

"I've already explained the reason," Havoc said.

Doc nodded. "Yep. But I still don't like it much."

The neighborhood in which the warehouse was located contained a few deserted business offices and similar storehouses. Most of the workers had departed for the day and traffic was sparse.

Captain Havoc considered the lack of pedestrians a plus. At least, he reasoned, they wouldn't have to worry about bystanders being accidentally hurt. He scrutinized the parking lot behind the warehouse, counting seven vehicles all told, six cars and a van. A frown creased his mouth. There must be other Brothers inside besides Mr. Bad and the one known as the Claw, which would make their job that much harder.

"Why are there no lights on?" Sparrow Hawk queried.

"Because they know we're after them and they're hidin' in the dark, tremblin' with fear," Lobo said, and snickered.

"They don't know we're on their trail," Doc stated.

The Clansman shrugged. "Then maybe they all went beddy-bye early. How should I know."

"I don't like it," Havoc declared. "It smells of a trap. They may not be expecting us, but they might be expecting the Barons. I wish we had more weapons." He drove into an alley to the east of the warehouse, bordering the parking lot, and braked.

"We could pull a Madsen and ram one of the doors with the car," Lobo suggested.

"No," Havoc responded. "Ramming plate-glass doors is one thing, but those on that building are probably reinforced with steel and as solid as a rock."

"Then how will we get in?" Sparrow questioned.

"We'll come up with a way," Havoc said confidently, turning off the ignition and killing the lights. He grinned. "We could always knock on the office door and claim we're selling Girl Scout cookies."

No one laughed.

"Who are the Girl Scouts?" Sparrow inquired.

"I didn't figure you California types were much good at scouting and trapping and such," Doc added.

"Are these Girl Scouts foxes?" Lobo wanted to know. "How about settin' me up on a date with one?"

Havoc sighed and climbed out, taking a M.A.C. 10 from the front seat and turning to face the warehouse and the parking lot. There were few streetlights in the industrial district. A full moon rising in the east provided pale illumination.

The others bailed out of the car.

"Want me to check out the warehouse?" Jag asked.

"We'll stick together for the time being," Havoc said, and looked at Lobo. "All except for you. You stay here with the Chevy."

"Say what?"

"You heard me."

"Why the hell should I stay here?" the Clansman replied indignantly.

"Because you were shot, remember?"

"I'm fine now," Lobo stated, and to emphasize his contention he reached up and swiftly removed the makeshift bandage.

"You're injured," Havoc reiterated. "You could become dizzy at any moment."

"He's always dizzy," Jag interjected.

"Up yours," Lobo snapped. "I'm not stayin' here and that's final."

"Yes, you are," Havoc stated.

"Oh, yeah? Who's going to make me?"

"Me."

"When did Blade die and Gallagher make you his replacement?" Lobo said angrily.

"Lighten up, Lobo," Jag commented. "Havoc is right and you know it."

"Yeah," Doc said. "We don't have time for this squabbling with Raphaela's life on the line."

The Clansman looked at each of them, then leaned against the car and folded his arms on his chest. "Fine. Be that way. If you chumps don't want me along, go by yourselves. Get wasted. See if I care."

"If we're not back in fifteen minutes, call the police,"

Havoc instructed, and ran toward the parking lot.

"Yeah. Sure," Lobo said, and watched his companions cross to the van and the six cars, then dash to the side of the loading platform where they were lost in the darkness. He grinned, waited a minute to be sure none of them would be looking back at him, and followed.

The concrete loading dock stood five feet high. Captain Havoc crouched in the inky gloom at its base and whispered instructions. "We'll split up here. Jag, you and Sparrow swing around to the right. Doc and I will take the left side. See if you can discover a way in. We'll meet out front near the office door."

"Be seeing you," Jag said, and slipped into the night with the Flathead right behind him.

"Maybe that big metal door is unlocked," Doc speculated.

"Even if it is, opening it would rouse the dead," Havoc said. "There's got to be another way." He ran along the dock until he reached the corner, then paused to scan the side of the warehouse. There was no sign of movement, no hint of light within. Where were the damn Brothers? Keeping low, he moved to the west, constantly surveying the windows for any hint of danger. When he came to the first barred-ground level window, he halted to inspect it. The bars were encased in the wall, impossible to remove without explosives or a blowtorch. He peered at the glass and discovered the reason no light was visible. Someone had spray-painted the inside of the window a dark blue or black. At the very edges a thin seam of light could be detected, but otherwise the warehouse appeared to be empty and deserted. He gazed upward, speculating on whether all the windows had been painted or just those on the ground floor.

Havoc continued westward, passing four more barred windows before he stopped at the far corner. He poked his head out and was surprised to find Jag and Sparrow had not yet arrived.

Doc eased alongside the officer. "Why don't we try that office door? It can't hurt."

Why not, indeed? Havoc sprinted to the door and pressed

his back to the wall. The hybrid and the Flathead had still not appeared. Leaning forward, he extended his left arm and gripped the doorknob lightly. At the bottom of the door faint rays of light were discernible.

"I'm ready," Doc whispered, cocking his Magnum.

Havoc began to turn the knob slowly, intending to open the door a mere hair if it wasn't locked. To his astonishment, the knob twisted easily. Too easily, as it turned out, for suddenly the door was thrown wide from within, jarring Havoc's arm and throwing him off balance. Before he could recover, an M-16 barrel was rammed into his ribs.

"Freeze or die, suckers!"

Brothers poured from the warehouse, seven of them in all, each armed with an assault rifle, each swinging his weapon to cover the officer and the Cavalryman.

Doc Madsen almost fired. He stepped away from the wall to give himself a clear shot even as the door opened, but in the instant he started to squeeze the trigger he saw the first gang member jab the M-16 into Havoc's side. He knew if he shot the Brother, the man might still get off a few rounds. If so, Havoc's life was forfeit. So superb were his reflexes, so coordinated his control of his hands, that he was able to refrain from firing, and by then it was too late to offer any resistance because the rest of the Brothers had emerged.

"Drop your guns!" the lead Brother directed. "Now!"

Reluctantly, his eyes smoldering, Doc lowered the Magnum to the ground.

Havoc eased his M.A.C. 10 downward until it rested near his feet.

"Thought you were pulling a fast one, huh, turkeys?" the spokesman said, and snorted. "We saw you jokers coming from the upstairs windows and Mr. Bad arranged this little reception."

"We're looking forward to seeing him," Havoc mentioned.

"Shut your face, honky," the Brother snapped, then glanced at another gang member. "Artie, take four guys and go find those two who were coming around the other side.

Remember, the boss wants 'em alive if possible."

"Got it, Spooner," Artie replied. He pointed at three other Brothers and they raced to the north corner.

Artie gouged the barrel into the officer. "Inside, asshole. And don't try no funny stuff."

His arms in the air, his features hardened in resentment of his own stupidity in being captured, Havoc stepped into the warehouse, glancing at the north corner as he did, one thought uppermost in his mind.

Where the hell were Jaguarundi and Sparrow Hawk?

"Hold it," Jag whispered when they were halfway along the north side of the structure.

"What is it, my brother?" Sparrow asked softly.

"I've got to go."

"What?"

"I have to take a leak."

"This is not the proper time for humor," the Flathead noted.

"Who's kidding?" Jag responded. "I've had to go since we left the condo, and that driving around didn't help my kidneys much." He took two strides from the wall and reached under his loincloth.

Sparrow looked both ways, then at the hybrid. "Can't you hold it in?"

"When a guy's got to go, he's got to go," Jag said, and began spraying the barren strip of land rimming the north side of the building. "Ahhhhh. Relief at last."

Sparrow heard the urine splattering the ground and inhaled a pungent scent that reminded him of the smell of mountain lion pee. He scrunched up his nose and held his breath, waiting impatiently for the hybrid to finish. The cat-man seemed to go on forever. Sparrow was finally compelled to take a breath, and the odor almost made him cough.

"There we go," Jag whispered, and hitched at his loincloth. He headed westward again, proceeding cautiously, his keen ears alert for the slightest sound.

"Would you do me a favor?" Sparrow requested.

"What's that?"

"The next time, stand downwind."

"Smart-ass."

Jag flexed his fingers as he neared the corner. He was still six feet away when he heard a sudden commotion from the front of the building, and alarmed for the safety of Havoc and Doc, he ran to the corner and stopped. A hasty glance revealed the pair partly ringed by armed Brothers.

"What's happened?" Sparrow asked, the words barely audible.

"They've been caught," Jag replied, weighing the implications. Was it possible the Brothers had seen them approach? If so, there would be gang members after Sparrow and him within seconds. "Come on," he prompted, and jogged away from the corner, retracing their route to the nearest barred window.

"What are we doing?" Sparrow asked.

"Planning a little surprise of our own," Jag answered. The lower edge of the window came to the height of his chest, and he reached up and took hold of two bars, testing them. They would resist even his bestial strength, but he had no intention of trying to break them. "Climb," he said, and immediately did so, clambering to the top of the bars and pressing flat against the wall.

Sparrow promptly followed suit, clamping his teeth on the hilt of his knife so his hands would be free.

Seconds later the drumming of running feet heralded the appearance of four Brothers at the northwest corner. They slowed, scanning the ground, searching for the two intruders they knew to be on the property.

"Where'd they go?" one of them asked.

"Maybe they went back toward the loading dock," suggested another.

"After 'em," said the Brother in the lead.

The four gang members dashed toward the rear, hugging the wall, their attention focused on the area in front of them and the space between the warehouse and the next building to the north. None of them gave the windows more than a cursory glance because they rightly believed the bars were unbreakable and no one could gain entry on the ground level.

Jag grinned as the quartet came underneath the bars, then launched himself into the air, his fingers curled in the shape of claws, eager to tear into the Brothers, and tear into them he did, his arms in motion the moment his feet plowed into the back of the foremost gang member. He raked his nails across the face of the second Brother, ripping the skin and lacerating the man's eyes, and used the back of the collapsing leader as a springboard. He vaulted and flipped, tucking his knees into his chest, and landed between the second and third Brother.

"My eyes!" the second man shrieked, his hands clasping his face.

His motions a blur, Jag grabbed the front of the third Brother's T-shirt and lifted the man into the air, then cast him at the fourth gang member, who was in the act of bringing his assault rifle to bear.

The first Brother had already recovered. He rose to his knees and twisted, aiming at the hybrid's furry back. Out of the corner of his eye he detected movement, and then a heavy body struck him on the chest and knocked him down. Dazed, he looked up to behold, of all things, an Indian. An Indian with a knife.

Sparrow speared his hunting knife straight into the gang member's heart, hearing the thud as the hilt hit the chest, and saw the Brother stiffen and gasp. He wrenched the blade out and spun, and not a foot away stood the Brother with the torn eyes.

"Help me!" the man screeched. "I can't see!"

His right arm whipping in an upward sweep, Sparrow sank the blade into the second man's neck at the base of the throat. Warm blood cascaded over his fingers and wrist, and he yanked the knife out again.

"No!" the Brother wailed, a crimson gusher gusting from his mouth. He tottered and dropped to his knees, blubbering in anguish, then fell forward and was still.

Sparrow went to assist his friend, but the battle was over. Jaguarundi was astride the last gang member, blood and gore coating his fingers and nails. He straightened and turned. "Are you okay?"

"Yes. And you?"

"I'm just getting warmed up. Someone was bound to have heard that bozo yelling. Grab a couple of weapons and let's go."

Sparrow hastily retrieved two M-16's, slung one over his left shoulder, and moved toward the corner. The hybrid was several feet in front of him, and Sparrow noticed that Jag had not picked up a gun. "Shouldn't you have a weapon too?" he asked.

"I do," Jaguarundi responded, and wagged his hands. "Ten of them."

Lobo squatted behind the van and scrutinized the loading dock. His teammates had disappeared a short while ago, and he debated whether to follow Havoc and Doc or Jag and Sparrow. As he peered at the rear of the warehouse he noticed a window to the left of the corrugated metal door, high up near the roof.

What if the Brothers had a lookout posted there?

The idea bothered Lobo. It meant his friends would be walking into a trap unless they were very careful. But Havoc was a professional soldier. Surely the captain would have reached the same conclusion. Even so, what choice would Havoc have had except to continue the operation? They needed weapons if they were to rescue Raphaela, and the weapons they wanted were inside that warehouse.

Maybe a distraction was in order.

Lobo scratched his head, trying to devise a suitable diversion, a scheme that might draw the Brothers out or at the very least lure their attention away from Havoc and the rest.

But what?

He gazed at the parked vehicles. If he had the keys, he could drive them onto the loading dock wall or something. *That* would really grab the Brothers' attention. Only he didn't have the keys, and he didn't know how to start a vehicle without them.

So what else could he do?

Lobo thought and thought, and after a bit grinned in delight at the inspiration he received.

"Yep.

This promised to be fun!

There were seven more armed Brothers, most attired in leather clothes or jeans and torn T-shirts, waiting inside when Havoc and Doc were ushered into the warehouse.

"Here's two of the bastards," the gang member named Spooner announced. He was a heavyset black with a styled Afro.

The two remaining Brothers from the ambush detail closed the door and posted themselves on either side.

"Where's Artie and the rest?" one of the seven inquired.

"I sent them after the others," Spooner replied.

"I noticed you didn't go with them."

Spooner glared at the speaker, then prodded Havoc with his M-16. "Keep moving, honky."

The captain glanced to the right and the left, studying the layout, seeking a means of turning the tables. To his left, wide metal stairs ascended to the second floor, and partly visible through a doorway was a darkened chamber. Only the lights on the bottom floor had been turned on. To the right was a small closed office.

Directly ahead stretched an enormous expanse of concrete floor. Crates and boxes had been stacked high against each wall, reaching almost to the ceiling. Solitary bulbs positioned at 20-foot intervals sufficed for lighting. Apparently no one bothered to clean very often because dust and litter dotted the concrete. Standing 40 feet from the door, near a short column of wooden crates, were the handsome guy and the one with the pincer.

Mr. Bad and the Claw.

Havoc strolled casually toward them, his eyes roving to the crates and boxes, reading the words someone had scrawled in red magic marker on the side of each one. Many of the words made no sense to him. CRYSTAL. SNEEZE. ZIG-ZAGS. But others he definitely recognized. M-16's. GRENADE LAUNCHERS. MORTARS. There were enough crates of arms to outfit an army.

"Hey, Boss!" Spooner called out. "Got two presents for you!"

The head of the Brothers and his hulking bodyguard advanced to meet them.

At that moment a loud screech sounded outside, on the north side of the building, and a man was heard crying, "My eyes!"

"What the hell!" Spooner blurted.

Mr. Bad halted and cocked his head. Several of his men started for the door, but he stopped them with an imperious gesture.

"That was Fritzy," Spooner said. "I'm sure of it."

Seconds later the same man shouted again. "Help me! I can't see!" Then there was a terrified "No!" Then silence.

"Should we go help them, Boss?" Spooner asked.

"And be cut down before you got two yards?" Mr. Bad replied sarcastically. "No, Spooner. We stay put until I get to the bottom of this." He walked up to Havoc and studied the officer's countenance, then glanced at the Cavalryman. "Neither of you are Barons."

"What was your first clue?" Havoc joked, and immediately regretted his brashness when Mr. Bad backhanded him across the mouth. He rocked with the blow but retained his footing.

"Don't open your mouth unless I tell you to open it," Mr. Bad stated harshly, and motioned at his bodyguard.

The Claw came over and extended his left arm, his metal pincer gleaming in the light. He opened and closed the pincer with a loud snap.

"Try to be funny again and I'll have Claw crush your balls to a pulp," Mr. Bad vowed.

Havoc held himself in check with a supreme effort. He could feel blood trickling from the corner of his mouth.

"I've seen these two guys before," the Claw declared.

"You have?"

"Yeah. Don't you remember? They were with that redheaded chick at the club."

Mr. Bad stared from one to the other. "Now that you mention it, I do remember them." He leaned toward Havoc.

"Who are you? What are you doing here?"

"The name is Havoc. Captain Mike Havoc."

"Captain?" Mr. Bad said, clearly confused. "You're in the military?"

"The Freedom Force."

Mr. Bad's eyes narrowed. "This is crazy. I've heard of the Force. Why the hell would you guys be muscling in on my action?"

Havoc didn't respond.

"I won't ask you again."

"Let me make him talk, Boss," the Claw said.

Captain Havoc braced for a beating, or worse. He wasn't about to tell them about Raphaela or the fact the Force had hit Mr. Bad's condo. For that matter, he wasn't about to tell them a thing. He thought of all the innocent blood that had been shed because of the two gangs, all the people whose lives had been destroyed by the drugs the Brothers and the Barons purveyed, and he decided to go down swinging, to take as many of them with him as he could.

"Knock yourself out," Mr. Bad said to his bodyguard.

The Claw grinned and elevated his pincer to eye level. "So you're a captain, huh? You must figure you're one tough dude."

"I can take you," Havoc stated.

The assembled Brothers cackled. Mr. Bad snorted and shook his head.

"Give me a fair fight and I'll prove it," Havoc declared boldly, hoping their cocky overconfidence would prove to be their undoing. If he could engage the Claw in hand-to-hand combat, he might be able to get near enough to one of the others to grab a weapon.

The Claw gazed at the officer, his forehead furrowed. "What do you say, Boss?"

"I say snip his ears off," Mr. Bad responded.

"You heard the man," the Claw said, and opened his pincer.

Havoc tensed, about to unleash a kick, when he heard the beating of boots on the metal stairs and a voice raised in alarm.

"Mr. Bad! Mr. Bad!"

The Brothers all turned their attention to the man rushing down the steps, a Spanish gang member wearing jeans and a brown vest.

"Calm down, Mescalito," Mr. Bad advised. "What's wrong?"

Mewscalito paused near the bottom and leaned on the rail. "It's the cars. Someone is at the cars."

"How do you know? What are they doing?"

"All the lights are on, and I could see a lot of men moving around."

"Were they Barons?"

"I couldn't tell, Mr. Bad. All I saw were a lot of men running in front of the headlights."

"Damn," Mr. Bad snapped, and scowled. "If they take out our wheels, we'll be stranded." He looked at Spooner. "Take everyone with you except two men to keep these clowns covered."

"Right away, Boss," Spooner responded, and indicated two of the Brothers. "You heard the man. You stay here and cover the prisoners." He wheeled and led a general dash to the office door.

Captain Havoc almost smiled. Here was his golden opportunity. The pair of Brothers left behind were standing closer to Doc Madsen. One of them had Doc's Magnum tucked under his belt.

"I don't like this," Mr. Bad remarked. "We're getting out of here."

"What about the soldier and the cowboy?" the Claw inquired.

"They no longer interest me. Kill them."

"As you wish." The Claw grinned at Havoc. "I'll make this as painless as possible."

"Don't do me any favors."

A sudden burst of gunfire erupted outside the office door. Men screamed and cursed. A full-scale war seemed to be in progress. The chattering of assault rifles and the booming of shotguns caused Mr. Bad, his bodyguard, and the pair of guards to swing toward the door in surprise. For only a few seconds they totally ignored their prisoners.

Which was all the time Havoc needed. He leaped into the air and executed a double flying kick, his left foot connecting with Mr. Bad's nose, his right striking the Claw's chin, the force of his blows sending both men reeling backwards. With almost ballet-like grace he landed in the *Zenkutsu-tachi,* the forward stance, and instantly pressed his attack, well aware that one of the guards could send a bullet into his back at any moment. He skipped forward and delivered a devastating roundhouse kick to the side of the Claw's face, knocking the bodyguard to one knee.

Mr. Bad had recovered and was reaching under his jacket, blood flowing from his nostrils.

Havoc nearly flinched when a shot rang out, the blasting of a heavy handgun, not an M-16. He ignored the gunshot and concentrated on his task, reaching Mr. Bad in two bounds and spinning, his right leg straight and rigid, his heel catching his foe on the left knee, shattering the kneecap with a loud snap.

A cry of pain tore from Mr. Bad's lips and he went down, still game, drawing a pistol from a shoulder holster.

Havoc drove his right hand in a vicious palm-heel thrust into Mr. Bad's chin, stunning the head man. But before he could finish his adversary off with a handsword chop to the neck, a vise clamped on his right shoulder and he was hurled backwards. Something tore through the fabric of his blue shirt and bit deep into his flesh, and then he was in the clear and staring at the Claw.

The bodyguard sneered and held out his bloody pincer.

And then three events occurred almost simultaneously. Havoc saw Mr. Bad aim the pistol at his chest, and he knew he was done for because he couldn't possibly reach the man before the trigger was pulled, and he was about to make a mad, desperate lunge when Mr. Bad suddenly looked past him at something or someone, and his eyes went wide as three shots thundered, three retorts from a revolver, the familiar *bam-bam-bam* of a certain Magnum, and Mr. Bad's forehead dissolved in a shower of skin and bones and crimson a millisecond before the impact catapulted him onto his back.

"*No!*" the Claw bellowed, insane with rage, and charged. He sprang at Havoc in a frenzy, slashing and swinging in reckless abandon.

Blocking and countering one blow after another, Havoc retreated several yards, his forearms stinging from the unyielding metal pincer, reacting on sheer instinct, relying on his years of training. Unbidden thoughts of Jimmy entered his head, thoughts of why his younger brother had enlisted in the Force, of why Jimmy had given his life in the line of duty. It had nothing to do with Blade, or the Warrior's decision to land in Canada. It had everything to do with serving a higher cause, with fighting for ideals and values worth dying for if need be. It had everything to do with putting an end to human garbage like Mr. Bad and the Claw, people who ruined the lives of others for their personal pleasure or gain. All these thoughts went through his mind in a flash, and the brief distraction cost him, enabling the Claw to score a hit, to tear open his left side.

But that was the last hit the Claw ever scored.

Havoc abruptly went berserk, raining a flurry of hand and foot blows, punching and chopping and stabbing, using his rock-hard fingers to their maximum advantage, driving the Claw backwards, connecting with a *Hitosashiyubi-ippon-ken,* a forefinger fist to the ribs that staggered the bodyguard, and then landing a piercing hand thrust to the stomach that doubled the Brother in half.

A red haze seemed to shroud Havoc's eyes as he continued his onslaught, employing a handsword face chop to send the Claw stumbling to the left. He closed in, and he dimly registered the bodyguard looking at him in stark amazement, but the next instant the vision was blotted out as he lanced his right index finger into the Claw's eye.

The bodyguard jerked his head back, exposing his throat.

Havoc never missed a beat. He whipped his right hand in a sword peak jab into the Claw's neck. Once. Twice. Three times he struck, and after the third strike the Claw gurgled and collapsed. Not satisfied, Havoc adopted the cat stance, ready to fight indefinitely if necessary, staring at the form sprawled at his feet in confusion, wondering why the man was simply lying there.

"He's dead, Mike."

The softly spoken words cut through the red haze and brought Havoc back to his senses. He blinked a few times and nudged the bodyguard with his right foot.

"Mike?"

The voice belonged to Jaguarundi, and Havoc turned to find the hybrid standing next to Sparrow and Doc Madsen. All three were regarding him with peculiar expressions.

"Are you okay?" Jag asked.

"I'm fine," Havoc mumbled, finally allowing his body to relax and his arms to drop to his sides. Weariness pervaded him from head to toe.

"We took care of the rest," Jag mentioned. "Caught most of them while they were going out the door, then Doc helped us out after he took care of the few in here."

"I see," Havoc said, his tone husky. "We did well. Blade will be proud of us."

Jag, Sparrow, and Doc were shocked when they saw tears form in the captain's eyes.

"Are you sure you're okay?" Jag queried.

"Fine," Havoc responded in a whisper. "Where's Lobo?"

"You told him to stay in the car, remember?"

"Oh. Yeah." Havoc straightened and inhaled deeply, then shuffled toward the door.

A figure suddenly appeared in the doorway. "Well, *there* you bozos are!" Lobo strolled inside, grinning happily. "Did it work or did it work?"

"What are you babbling about?" Jag rejoined.

"My plan to confuse these turkeys," Lobo said. "I turned on all their car headlights and kept running around the vehicles, thinking they would figure that they were under attack. I wanted to keep their attention off you guys. Did it work?"

"It worked," Doc disclosed. "You probably saved Havoc and me from being killed."

"I did?" Lobo puffed out his chest and beamed. "See? I knew you guys couldn't manage without me. I'm the brains of this outfit. You need me to bail you out when the going gets tough. Maybe I should talk to General Gallagher about taking over from Blade. I can teach that bag of wind a—"

"Lobo?" Havoc interrupted.

"Yeah?"

"Shut the hell up."

The Clansman, indignant, opened his mouth to respond. He took a good look at the officer's face and abruptly changed his mind.

CHAPTER NINETEEN

Blade came over the north wall when a cloud veiled the grinning face of the moon and cast the landscape in temporary total darkness. To someone of his stature the ten-foot wall hardly qualified as an obstacle. He took a running leap and vaulted upward, his brawny hand catching on the outer edge, then hoisted himself onto his stomach. A hasty inspection revealed a half acre devoted to a lush garden replete with ferns and high trees, illuminated by the light from several posts positioned at strategic intervals. He slid off the wall, twisted, and alighted on his feet.

"Did you hear something?"

The surly voice froze the Warrior in a crouch. He estimated the speaker must be 15 or 20 feet to his right. A glance at the sky confirmed that the cloud would soon be drifting eastward and the moon would add its distant brilliance to the glow from the lamps. He was at the base of the wall, in the open, and the Barons might spot him unless he could find cover.

Not six yards away, straight ahead, rose a bushy plant,

its thin leaves rising to a height of five feet and then drooping almost to the ground, willowlike.

Blade flattened and crawled to the bush, carefully parted the leaves, and concealed himself at its base. None too soon.

"I tell you I heard something."

"You probably heard a frog fart."

The Warrior peered between the leaves and spotted a pair of armed Barons approaching from the west. One held an M-16, the other a shotgun.

"How would you know?" the shotgun wielder snapped. "You don't know nothin' about animals."

"And you do?"

"I know I didn't hear a frog fart. They sound like popcorn popping and this was different."

"You're so full of shit it's dripping out your ears."

Blade placed his hands on the hilts of his Bowies. He had removed the knives from under his fatigue pants before launching his assault on the Barons' stronghold and strapped the sheaths to his belt. After he returned to the Force compound—*if* he returned—he intended to have a long talk with General Gallagher about the policy of no weapons when in L.A. Unless the policy was changed, he'd never enter the city again.

The two Barons halted next to the wall and scanned the garden. After a minute the man carrying the M-16 sighed and said, "I don't see a thing. This is a frigging waste of our time."

"Don't let Bennie hear you say that."

"Mr. High and Mighty? Boy, the boss makes him second-in-command and he starts acting like he's God."

"Bennie can't afford to screw up. Don't forget what happened to Barney."

"Barney was a jerk."

They started to walk to the east, their vigilance slightly reduced.

Amateurs, Blade thought, and surged from under the plant, drawing his Bowies as he rose, the blades gleaming, his arms tensed to strike.

To their credit, the two Barons heard the rustle of the leaves and tried to rotate. They were only partly successful.

The Warrior reached them in two strides and speared his knives up and in, sinking each one into an exposed neck before either Baron could turn, eliciting a terrified cry from the man carrying the M-16 and a grunt from the other Baron. He quickly released the hilts, took hold of each man by the back of the head, and slammed their foreheads together to forestall further noise.

Wheezing and spitting blood, the shotgun-wielder toppled over, but the Baron with the M-16 tried to bring his weapon to bear on the giant.

Blade batted the barrel aside and swung a brutal uppercut to the man's chin, his prodigious might breaking the Baron's jaw, splintering a dozen teeth, and shattering the left cheekbone.

The Baron dropped.

Crouching, the Warrior surveyed the garden but detected no movement. Working swiftly, he pulled his Bowies out and wiped them on the pants of the shotgun-wielder, then slid them into their sheaths and took hold of the shotgun and the M-16. Now, as Lobo would say, he was ready to rock and roll. He slung the M-16 over his right shoulder and advanced in a beeline toward the mansion. After ten yards he came to a gravel-covered path winding among the plants and took it, his boots crunching lightly on the stones.

"Gage, is that you?"

Another pair of Barons appeared on the left, coming around a maple tree.

"Sure isn't," Blade replied, and shot them, working the slide action on the Mossberg Model 3000 with lightning rapidity. The two shots boomed almost as one, and both Barons were struck in the chest and sent sailing backwards, dead before they hit the ground.

All hell broke loose.

Blade raced toward the mansion, listening to the outbreak of yells and curses all around him, and wondered how many Barons were on the premises.

A stocky Baron dressed all in leather and carrying a Heckler and Koch HK-93 crashed through a row of shrubbery on the right, saw the giant, and cut loose.

The Warrior was already in motion, diving for the damp ground and rolling as the rounds from the HK-93 smacked into the earth within inches of his head. He fired as he rolled, the shotgun barrel slanted upward at the Baron, and the blast caught the gang member in the head and exploded his face outward in a shower of skin, blood, teeth, and bone.

Five down.

How many more to go?

Blade pushed to his feet and dashed to the dead Baron. Nearby lay the HK-93. He tossed the shotgun into the bushes and grabbed the HK-93 with his left hand while unslinging the M-16 with his right. He tucked both weapons against his ribs to absorb the recoil, a finger on each trigger, and resumed his attack, walking brazenly along the path. There was ample cover available, but he opted for the direct approach for two reasons. First, the Barons knew he was on the grounds and would be converging on him in force. He'd rather take the fight to them, put them on the defensive, than skulk in the bushes and try to pick them off one by one. Second, and most important, time was a crucial factor. Every moment of delay increased the likelihood that Raphaela would be harmed, if she hadn't been before he arrived.

So where are you, you bastards?

The Warrior came abreast of a flower garden, the fragrant aroma tingling his nose, and on the opposite side three Barons materialized.

"Here he is!" one of them shouted.

Blade squeezed both triggers, combining the firepower of both the M-16 and the HK-93, and swung them from side to side, sending a withering hail of lead into the trio. Only one of the Barons succeeded in getting off a few rounds, and the shots went wild and destroyed a three-foot section of flowers.

Just as the retorts of the guns died away, a piercing scream arose from the bowels of the mansion, wafting eerily on the wind, the unmistakable scream of someone the Warrior knew.

Raphaela!

Throwing caution aside, Blade plunged through the vegetation toward a sturdy oak door on the north side of the mansion. He dreaded the thought that the Barons might kill Raphaela before he could reach her, and in his haste to find her he became uncharacteristically careless.

The oak door was closed but unguarded.

Blade leaped over a rose bush and came to a narrow strip of unadorned grass. He increased his speed, his gaze riveted on the door, and when he was only six feet from his goal he detected motion out of his right eye and spun.

Too late.

A solitary Baron got off three rounds from a Ruger Mini-14 Carbine.

A scorching firebrand seared a groove in Blade's right side, racking his torso with excruciating agony, and he fell to the dank earth and stayed there, not moving a muscle, gritting his teeth to suppress the pain he felt, hoping the Baron would come close to verify the presumed kill. Stealthy footsteps sounded, drawing slowly nearer. The M-16 was pinned under his right side, but the HK-93 was still clutched in his left hand, the barrel slanted toward the ground.

The footsteps halted.

Would the man fire a few more times for good measure? Blade's skin prickled as he waited for the Baron to do something. The seconds dragged by, and then the steps were much closer and a hard object prodded the Warrior's left shoulder. Blade went with the prod, rolling onto his back and elevating the HK-93 at the startled youth standing above him. He shot at a range of less than an inch, and the heavy slugs tore through the gang member's upper chest and flung the man to the grass.

Go! Blade's mind urged.

There was no time to inspect the wound. He had to trust that his blood loss would be minimal and that he could hold out until after he found Raphaela. Grimacing from the anguish, he rose and moved to the oak door. A twist of the knob revealed it had been locked.

No problem.

The Warrior took a step backwards, then kicked, planting

his right combat boot on the panel next to the lock, cracking the wood and making a noise undoubtedly heard in every room in the mansion.

It couldn't be helped.

Blade smashed the door again with his boot, and this time the panel splintered and the door swung inward, revealing a narrow hallway.

There were no Barons in sight.

Leveling the assault rifles, Blade entered warily, his gray eyes darting from room to room as he moved deeper and deeper into the Barons' sanctum sanctorum. The complete silence was unnerving. Not even an insect stirred. But he knew the Barons were in there somewhere, ready to spring a trap.

Let them try!

He reached a junction and halted, debating which of the branches he should follow.

Another appalling scream rent the air, seeming to originate far down the hallway on the right.

Blade raced along the corridor, oblivious to the wound in his side, thinking only of Raphaela, of the naive woman he had allowed to remain on the Force against his better judgment, of the woman whose life, literally, was in his hands. He'd already lost five Force members, and he wasn't about to lose another one. He'd die first.

The corridor abruptly angled to the left and widened, and he mustered all the speed he could, his long legs flying, passing many more rooms, all of them empty. The silence had again descended and he had no way of telling if he was still going in the right direction. Just when he thought the corridor might go on forever, he came to the bottom of a flight of stairs and stopped.

Now which way?

Acting on impulse rather than a seasoned deliberation, Blade started up the stairs, taking them one at a time, his head cocked to detect any telltale squeaks or clicks or anything that would indicate a trap. The remaining Barons had to know he was now in the mansion. They also assuredly knew he would be drawn to Raphaela's cries like a moth to flame. Which meant the trap must be somewhere ahead.

It was.

Blade took two more steps and then froze when a strange *thump* sounded. Then another. And another. Perplexed, he gazed upward, his blood transforming to ice when he spied the metallic sphere bouncing down the stairs toward him.

A hand grenade!

The Warrior reverted to sheer reflexive action, dropping the M-16 and the HK-93 and gripping the railing.

Thump.

Blade vaulted over the railing, his rippling muscles propelling him in a high arc.

Thump.

The sound brought goosebumps to his flesh. He alighted on the balls of his feet, took two quick strides, and flung himself forward, his arms over his head for protection.

The hand grenade detonated with a tremendous explosion, rocking the mansion walls, blowing a gaping crater in the stairs and showering jagged pieces of wood and carpet in all directions.

Blade was almost to the floor when the concussion buffeted him, sending him tumbling end over end for a dozen yards, jarring his injured side, causing him to collide with the walls on both sides, until he came to rest on his stomach, the wind knocked out of him, engulfed in a swirling haze of smoke and tiny wood chips. His ears rang, and for several seconds he couldn't hear a sound. Then he heard words.

"—get the son of a bitch?"

"I think so."

"Teach him to mess with the Barons."

The Warrior struggled to his knees and shook his head, striving to clear the mental cobwebs. The Barons would spot him once the cloud dissipated. He stood, his legs shaky, and walked several feet.

"I can't see a damn thing!"

"Shut your mouth and keep looking."

Blade leaned on the right-hand wall for support. His strength was returning swiftly. Several yards ahead appeared an open door, and he scooted to the doorway and ducked inside, chagrinned to discover he'd slipped into a linen closet.

"Let's check the hallway."

There was no time to seek another hiding place. The Warrior stared at the shelves piled high with towels and sheets, frowning. A mouse would find it difficult to secret itself in such a small closet, so how could *he* expect to elude the Barons?

"Shoot to kill."

"You don't have to tell me twice."

The two Barons were getting very close! Blade used the only option available under the circumstances. He slid behind the closet door, pressed his back to the wall, drew his Bowies, and waited expectantly.

Would they peek behind the door?

"There's no body. We must have missed him," a Baron said softly.

"How? We had that sucker dead to rights."

The Warrior guessed the duo were within a few feet of his hiding place. He held his breath and looked through the crack between the door and the jamb. If they spotted him, he'd need to move fast.

They did.

A Baron suddenly stepped into the doorway and scanned the shelves. He was about to leave, and had even twisted and taken a half-step, when he glanced at the crack, his eyes narrowing, then widening in alarm.

Blade shoved the door, using both arms, sweeping it around and catching the Baron full in the face, the door acting like a huge club, hurling the man across the hall and into the wall. He yanked the door open, and there was the Baron, sagging on one knee and trying to bring an AK-47 to bear.

A second Baron abruptly stepped into view between the closet and the first man, apparently intending to aid his companion but instead aiding the Warrior. The Baron glanced at his companion, then at the closet.

The Warrior pounced, his powerful leg muscles driving him into the nearest Baron, and they both crashed down on the first Baron. For a moment Blade had them both pinned, and he sank his Bowie into the chest of the man under him, stabbing for the heart and hitting his target. He swung his left arm up and over the Baron, at the face of the man on the bottom of the pile, and the tip lanced into the gang member's right eye.

The Baron on the bottom screeched.

Blade straightened, drawing both bloody Bowies with him. The Baron on top rolled off, still breathing but almost gone, crimson spurting from his nose and mouth as he trembled violently, uncovering his companion. The second man had a hand pressed to his ruptured eye and was endeavoring to rise. Blade imbedded both knives to their hilts in the Baron's torso and held on as the man thrashed and kicked and eventually expired.

Now to find Raphaela.

He yanked his blades out and headed for the stairs. The grenade had blown the middle section to bits. He climbed as far as he could, sheated his Bowies, then leaped, grabbing the upper section of rail and gaining a foothold on a buckled step. In a smooth motion he pulled himself onto firm footing and sprang to the landing.

Again silence enveloped the mansion.

Blade drew his knives and moved along the corridor, his anxiety mounting. Where were they holding Raphaela? Why had she screamed? She might be naive, but she had impressed him as having a certain resiliency and inner toughness that would serve her in good stead in a crisis. What could the—

"You must be Blade."

The booming voice snapped the Warrior's attention to a room on the right, a bedroom occupied by two people. Standing alongside the bed, a Colt Delta Elite 10MM in his right hand, was an immense tank of a man dressed in an ebony suit. The gun wasn't pointed at the Warrior. It was aimed at the figure on the bed.

Raphaela.

Blade straightened and took a step forward, his fury rising at the sight of her tear-streaked features. She lay on her back, her arms bound behind her, rope binding her ankles, and cast a pleading, pitiable expression at him. The beige shirt she wore had been torn open, partly exposing her breasts to view, revealing red welts on her skin. He raised his Bowies, about to spring.

"If you do, this charming lady will die," the man in the suit warned. "Kindly drop those knives of yours on the floor. Now."

What choice did he have? Blade let the Bowies fall and walked calmly into the bedroom, halting just inside the doorway. "Let her go."

"What? And relinquish my trump card? You must be kidding?"

"Are you Owsley?"

"I am, sir. I'm flattered that you've heard of me."

"Until tonight I had no idea you even existed," Blade said flatly, his eyes locked on Raphaela's, trying to reassure her with his gaze.

"Really?" Owsley shrugged. "And here I thought I had acquired a modicum of fame."

Blade glanced at the head Baron. "What's this all about? Why did you kidnap Raphaela? Why did you attack the Force?"

"You won't believe me if I tell you."

"Try me."

Owsley sighed and waved the barrel of the Colt at Raphaela. "Kidnapping her was a mistake, an accident."

"An accident?" Blade repeated skeptically.

"I told you that you wouldn't believe me," Owsley said. "My men were supposed to abduct another woman named Gloria Mundy. Instead, they grabbed this luscious person by mistake."

Blade's eyebrows arched. A mistake? This whole episode had been the result of a mistake? "If it was an accident, like you say, then why didn't you simply release her?"

Owsley shook his head. "I knew you would show up eventually, and I needed a bargaining chip in case you got this far." He paused. "My compliments, sir. Every word they've written about you in the papers is true."

"I'm sorry, Blade," Raphaela interjected. "He made me scream to lure you up here. He—he . . ." She paused, tears flowing, and took a breath. "He hurt me."

Blade took a casual step closer to the leader of the Barons, doing his best to suppress his seething emotions. "You *hurt* her?"

"I gave her a little squeeze," Owsley replied, and smirked. "And I intend to give her more after I dispose of you."

"You're scum. Do you know that?"

Owsley stiffened. "There's no need to get personal." He nodded at the carpet. "Lay down with your arms extended, and no unorthodox moves or I will put a bullet in this vixen's brain."

Blade started to comply, bending forward, his arms at his sides. He planned to rush the Baron and rely on his speed to avoid a slug in the head, knowing his chance of success was extremely slim, but he suddenly received unexpected assistance from Raphaela.

The Molewoman drew her legs up to her chest and lashed out with her combat boots, striking Owsley's gun hand and swatting the Colt aside.

In a twinkling the Warrior leaped, his outstretched hands closing on Owsley's gun arm, his momentum bearing both of them to the bed. He felt Raphaela squirming under him, and then he rolled to the left, taking Owsley with him, and together they crashed onto the floor.

"Damn you!" Owsley hissed, and drove his left knee at the Warrior's groin.

Blade shifted and the knee hit him in the inner thigh, causing intense pain. He clamped his right hand on Owsley's throat and squeezed, his huge arm bulging, the veins on his temples standing out.

Mouthing an inarticulate grunt, Owsley let go of the Colt, tore his arm from the Warrior's grasp, and slugged Blade on the chin. To his surprise, his blow appeared to have no effect.

Blade felt the punch but ignored it. He focused all of his awesome might into his right hand, squeezing, ever squeezing, constricting his fingers on the Baron's neck. A blistering, irresistible rage had gripped his soul, and any semblance of self-control had been lost.

Unaccustomed to being bested in combat by any man,

Arthur Owsley gasped for air and battered the Warrior's cheek and jaw. When his punches failed to produce any result, he altered his strategy. He was lying partly under the Warrior, at an angle, and he bucked his legs and heaved, flinging his opponent from him at the same moment he wrenched on the hand strangling his throat. His maneuver worked, freeing him momentarily, and he leaped to his feet.

Blade rolled and stood, but he was a millisecond too slow. An express train seemed to ram into him, sending him tottering backwards, his arms flailing for support. His hands hooked onto the doorjamb, and for an instant he was suspended in the doorway.

Owsley charged again, his head lowered, a snorting bull intent on stomping the Warrior at all costs. His head butted into Blade's stomach as his arms looped around the giant's waist, and they both went down with Owsley on top.

Now it was Blade's turn to deliver a barrage of fists to his enemy's face, and he succeeded in forcing Owsley from him.

Both men jumped erect.

Owsley wiped a hand across his bloody mouth, and sneered. "You're the toughest mother I've ever tackled."

"And the last," Blade said.

"You think so?" Owsley responded, and assumed a boxing posture. "Why don't we do this like gentlemen?"

"Because there's only one gentleman here," Blade said, baiting him. He adopted a boxing stance of his own, glancing once over his right shoulder to ensure there were no Barons behind him.

Owsley saw and understood. "You bested all the rest. Now it's only you and me."

"Whenever you're ready."

"Then let's do it."

They clashed, exchanging a flurry of blows, jabs and hooks and crosses, blocking and ducking and clinching, both men supremely skilled, both endowed with exceptional strength and stamina. When their punches landed, they jarred the other man. Despite the Warrior's height advantage, the battle was a contest of equals.

Blade was impressed. He had fought countless foes during his action-filled lifetime, fought them armed or unarmed, fought them using wrestling, the martial arts, boxing, and other techniques, and few were the opponents who could rival Arthur Owsley. The man gave as good as he got.

Owsley aimed a right cross at the Warrior.

Parrying with an inside forearm block, Blade countered, delivering a straight right to Owsley's bulky body that rocked the Baron on his heels.

Instantly Owsley lashed out with a left jab, connecting on the Warrior's jawbone.

Dazed, Blade retaliated with a left hook, scoring a hit over the Baron's right eye, breaking the skin and starting a flow of blood.

Owsley blinked and retreated several strides, wiping his right sleeve on the cut, trying to staunch the crimson rivulet.

The Warrior pressed his advantage, closing in again, and as he passed the bedroom door he glanced in and saw Raphaela on the floor, rolling toward the doorway. Although he was puzzled and fleetingly wondered what she could possibly hope to accomplish, there was no time to ponder the matter. He traded blows with Owsley again, the two of them slugging it out with no holds barred.

For over a minute the battle continued.

Two minutes.

And then Blade gained the upper hand. Two jabs to the cut over Owsley's eye opened the wound even more, and the pouring blood restricted the Baron's field of vision.

Owsley never even saw the haymaker.

The Warrior swung his arm in a wide loop, his granite knuckles slamming into the side of the Baron's head with the force of a pile driver. Owsley tottered, his arms dropping, and Blade planted a right on the tip of the man's nose, then a left on the chin.

Grunting, Owsley staggered and sluggishly lifted his arms to defend himself. He had lost and he knew it, but he refused to quit. His lips were split, his face puffy.

Blade paused. His rage had evaporated during their fight, leaving a lingering resentment and anger. He still wanted to pound the Baron to a pulp, but his self-control had reasserted itself and he felt inclined to take the man into custody for the authorities.

At that moment the shots rang out, four of them in quick succession, and four holes blossomed in Arthur Owsley's visage, two in the sloping forehead and two near the nose. He flung his arms out and swayed, took a lurching step to the right, and toppled with a resounding crash.

Blade turned slowly.

She stood a few feet away, the Colt clenched in both hands, the tears all gone, her features hard and spiteful, her nostrils flaring. "Never again," she said softly, the two words encompassing the full gamut of human suffering and sorrow, denoting a hidden meaning in the profound tone with which they were uttered.

The Warrior lowered his arms and said nothing.

EPILOGUE

"Lobo says you wanted to see me, sir?"

Blade placed his hands on the hilts of his Bowies, then gazed idly at the azure sky overhead. He stood outside the command bunker, savoring the peace and quiet. "Yes, I do."

"What about?" Raphaela asked. She had on fatigues, and her boots had been spit-shined until the tips gleamed.

The Warrior stared into her eyes. "How are you feeling?"

"Fine, sir."

"You haven't said very much since you shot that Baron."

Raphaela shrugged. "What's to say? He had it coming."

"I agree."

"Anything else, sir?"

"What's with all the 'sirs'?"

"As you've been trying to get through our thick skulls, this is a military unit. It's about time I behaved in a military fashion," Raphaela replied.

Blade studied her, his forehead creasing. "And you're sure everything is okay?"

"Couldn't be better."

L. A. STRIKE

"There's nothing you'd like to talk about?"

Raphaela's lips parted, as if she were about to reply, but she looked at the bunker and shook her head.

"Nothing at all?" Blade pressed her.

"No."

"Fair enough. But if you ever feel the need to shoot the breeze, you know where to find me."

A sincere smile curved her mouth upward and she nodded. "I'll keep that in mind, sir."

"That'll be all," Blade said, and watched her walk off to join Lobo, Doc, Sparrow, and Jag. They were all taking a brief break before they started on their unarmed combat lesson for the day. He heard footsteps and turned to find Captain Havoc hauling one of the mats they would use during the session. "I'll give you a hand," he offered.

"That's okay, sir," the officer responded. "I can manage."

"How are your injuries?"

"To tell the truth, I hardly notice them," Havoc said. He deposited the mat and knelt to unravel it on the ground.

"Do you mind if I ask you a question?"

Havoc looked up. "Certainly not, sir."

"What was that business yesterday with General Gallagher? I saw the two of you over by the VTOL hangar. He was waving a newspaper and seemed to be chewing you out."

"You know the general," Havoc answered cryptically. "He gets flustered easily."

"Was he flustered about anything I should know?"

"No, sir," Havoc answered. "He was excited over that story about us being heroes for wiping out the Brothers and the Barons."

Back to square one, Blade thought, and sighed. No, not exactly. Because now he was certain that General Gallagher was up to something. What, he had no idea. But he'd find out sooner or later, and the general had better not be up to his old tricks or there would be a reckoning.

And what about the Molewoman?

Blade stared at her without being obvious about his interest.

He'd seen the stark inner torment reflected on her face when she shot Owsley, and he suspected she harbored a deep, terrible secret that she would only reveal under duress. So now he had two members of the team he needed to watch like the proverbial hawk.

"Hey, dude!" Lobo called out. "How about if we skip the martial-arts jive today? A lean, mean, fightin' machine like me doesn't need this crap. And I could really use a nap."

Blade shook his head.

Make that three.

**In the beginning, there was *Endworld*.
Now, there's...**

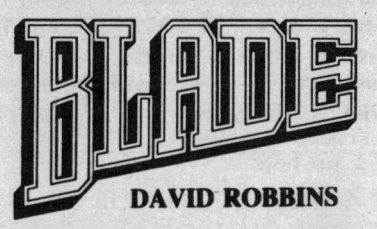

BLADE

DAVID ROBBINS

The high-action companion series to *Endworld*.

The hero of Leisure's post-nuclear adventure stars in a new series that packs more power than an H-bomb. Named for the razor-sharp Bowies that never left his side, Blade was the last hope for a ravaged civilization.

BLADE #1: FIRST STRIKE
____2760-7 $2.95US/$3.95CAN

BLADE # 2: OUTLANDS STRIKE
____2774-7 $2.95US/$3.95CAN

**LEISURE BOOKS
ATTN: Customer Service Dept.
276 5th Avenue, New York, NY 10001**

Please send me the book(s) checked above. I have enclosed $ _____
Add $1.25 for shipping and handling for the first book; $ .30 for each book thereafter. No cash, stamps, or C.O.D.s. All orders shipped within 6 weeks. Canadian orders please add $1.00 extra postage.

Name _____

Address _____

City _____ State _____ Zip _____
Canadian orders must be paid in U.S. dollars payable through a New York banking facility.   ☐ Please send a free catalogue.

SPEND YOUR LEISURE MOMENTS WITH US.

Hundreds of exciting titles to choose from—something for everyone's taste in fine books: breathtaking historical romance, chilling horror, spine-tingling suspense, taut medical thrillers, involving mysteries, action-packed men's adventure and wild Westerns.

SEND FOR A FREE CATALOGUE TODAY!

Leisure Books
Attn: Customer Service Department
276 5th Avenue, New York, NY 10001